FAR and AWAY

Forced Journey: The Saga of Werner Berlinger

by

Rosemary Zibart

Cover Illustration by

George Lawrence

Kinkajou Press
Albuquerque, New Mexico
www.apbooks.net

Dedication

To Sister Sandra Smithson with love and appreciation.

To all the generations of children and to every child who has made that journey to find a new life and a safe home.

Foreword

It is a fact that approximately 1,400 unaccompanied children came to the United States during the years 1934 to 1941. These children from Germany, Austria, and Czechoslovakia were fleeing the Nazi regime. It is also a fact that many of these children became teachers, lawyers, doctors, engineers. One even became a rock star and another a Nobel Prize winner. What is little known is how these children reacted to being forced to leave their parents and family behind and to grow up in the United States, in many cases never to see one or both parents again. On the one hand, there was little that they could do to control their lives until they reached America's shores. On the other hand, once they had arrived here, they were pretty much on their own, and that's the basis for the fascinating tale spun by Rosemary Zibart in *Forced Journey*.

It is a challenging task, considering the range of ages and backgrounds of these young boys and girls, to distill their stories into the saga of Werner Berlinger, but Ms. Zibart has done so with empathy and understanding. It is not only an interesting read, but there were many times in the story when I felt that what happened to Werner was what had happened to me.

Henry Frankel
President
One Thousand Children

"*What you standing there gawking for?*"

A rough-looking young man with dirty blond hair spoke to Werner. The boy had paused a moment on the edge of town to gaze at a sign with an arrow: *Hamburg, 64 kilometers.* Then he'd become stuck on the spot. Scared. Afraid to take the first step and leave behind everything he knew and cared about.

"Better get moving, if you want to get somewhere before dark," the fellow declared loudly. His clothes were as shabby as Werner's, but warmer. He looked several years older, 16 or 17 at least, and much sturdier, a farm worker, perhaps. He started walking with long strides. Werner fell in beside him, trying to keep up.

"I call myself Gunther," the fellow said, glad to have a traveling companion. "You know why there's so many people on the road, don't ya?"

Werner glanced around – the road was filled with people, mostly men, traveling in both directions.

"It's war again," declared Gunther. "That's what it is." He explained how he had heard on the radio that Germany had marched into Poland the day before, September 1, 1939. It had been a big success for the Nazis, he claimed. They'd flattened the Polish military.

"Those poor Polacks didn't have a chance," snorted the young man. "German soldiers are the best in the world, ain't they?" Werner didn't dare say a word, but the guy didn't seem to notice.

"I'm heading to Hamburg myself to sign up

as a soldier," Gunther announced proudly. "My father don't want me in the army. And Mother, she cried buckets. But it's my life, ain't it? And I'm no sissy." He puffed out his chest and showed off his big arm muscles.

He didn't ask the boy's name and Werner didn't volunteer it. He knew that he needed to be careful. If Gunther suspected he was Jewish, what might he do? Somebody so gung-ho for the German army could be very dangerous. Father had warned, "Speak to as few people as possible." Werner knew he was far safer on his own. So he was glad when Gunther found a more talkative young man and moved on.

Still, Gunther had gotten Werner moving and had set a fast pace. He was grateful for that. He had never traveled so far on his own. Every step carried him farther from Father and his sister, Bettina. His heavy boots were covered with mud, weighing them down and scraping his sockless feet raw. But he had to travel 64 kilometers in just three days. Then go even farther – a ship, an ocean, a voyage to an unknown land.

But Werner at least had a goal – get a foothold in America – a place to live, a home. Then Father had promised that he and Werner's little sister would follow. This dimly burning ember of hope lit the boy's path....

Chapter One

"Werner, Werner Berlinger," called Frau Schutz, matron of the orphanage.

"Uh-oh," Werner muttered to his friends.

It was late August. Rain had fallen for three straight days. The grey skies and chill in the air meant winter was not far off. Their bones ached from being inside all day and doing nothing. The boys had lapped up some thin gruel for breakfast. Then they had started playing checkers, with Werner winning, as usual.

He wondered why Frau Schutz was calling his name. Was it because the night before he had snuck into the kitchen? Had someone snitched on him? He glanced around at his buddies, Victor, Sammel, Lutz, and Mandel. Not one of them, surely.

Punishment at the orphanage was no joke. Frau Schutz made the children stand in a dark closet for hours or miss dinner. Missing out on food was even worse than standing in the dark. Though even when they ate, it wasn't much. Some watery soup and a little stale crummy bread, the kind the baker throws out if he can't sell it.

Germany's ruler, Adolf Hitler, had made his opinion clear. The more Jewish orphans (or sick or blind or aged or handicapped people) that starved to death, the better. So children in the orphanage were hungry all the time. Werner didn't remember one day or one hour of one day when his stomach wasn't growling. Often he got in trouble for stealing food – a piece of wormy cheese or fatty meat. Not worth stealing unless you're starving.

He strolled over to Frau Schutz, trying to seem bold but

expecting the worst. She surprised him. "Your father has written," she said. "He instructs me to send you home."

Werner's mouth dropped open. He stared at her like a little kid, not a scrawny twelve-year-old. Home? Home? He was finally going home?

He glanced down the hallway at his buddies. Most kids at the orphanage didn't have a parent but he did. And he had wanted – dreamed – of this news for a whole year.

"I'm glad your father wants you home, Werner," Frau Schutz said warmly. "You know the way, don't you?"

He nodded. She wasn't a bad person, he thought, just worn out, like a coin that's been passed around too long. She didn't like to punish the boys for stealing food, but there wasn't enough for everyone and so no child could get extra.

Werner stumbled down the hall, barely glancing at his friends. Still, they followed as he entered the long narrow room where their cots stood in a row. He knelt and reached underneath for the small wooden box with his things. Hands trembling, he took out the contents – a pencil, a little notebook and a precious photograph of his mother. Her soft round face and kind eyes smiled up at him as always. The picture was smudged from the many tears that had splashed on the fading print in the years since she had died. He carefully put the picture in his pocket, then dumped the other stuff and a few clothes into a worn knapsack.

"Ya going some place?" asked Lutz Chaimen in a squeaky voice. Such a little guy, yet he wanted to go too, and Werner wished he could take him.

"Home," Werner muttered, without looking up, so he wouldn't see the envy in the small boy's eyes.

Minutes later, ready to leave, he gave Lutz a squeeze, feeling the sharp bones beneath his skin. Victor, Sammel, and Mandel were closer to his age, so he just nodded to them, not sure what to say. The boys had shared so many moments, haunted by hunger and loneliness, they were like brothers in a ghost family.

"You're not gonna finish the game?" Lutz trailed him down the dim hallway to the heavy front door.

"Nah, not today." Werner paused and reached deep into his pocket. Months ago, he had discovered a large green and black marble in the dirt at the corner of the playground. He hadn't told a soul, fearing it would be stolen. Now he handed the marble to Lutz, glad to see a smile flash across the youngster's face.

Moments later, he was running down the road away from the orphanage. He didn't glance back, but murmured a quick prayer. *Please, God, please, help Lutz and the other boys get out too.*

Then he recalled how he had gotten to that dismal place.

Chapter Two

It was a year ago and he was simply walking home. But they had spied him from across the street, a gang of troublemakers – the *Hitler Jugend* – teenage boys who tried to act as stupid and mean as adult Nazis. Often they had chased Werner down the street. Usually he outraced them, but not that day.

"Hey, big nose," said a young tough, twice as a big as Werner. The sturdy blond boy twisted Werner's arm while pushing a piece of chalk into his other hand.

"Write on the sidewalk," he commanded, "*I am an ugly Jew-boy.*" Werner's hand shook so much the scrawl was barely readable. Still, the boys in brown uniforms howled with laughter. Then they released him and Werner slinked home, hot with shame.

That night he wet the bed like a baby. It wasn't the first time he had woken up with sheets damp and smelling of pee. His father said nothing in the morning. But while helping Werner change the bed, his face was grey, his shoulders hunched.

An hour later, Werner's eight-year-old sister, Bettina, pestered him about something. He started yelling, then grabbed Minnie, a beautiful doll with a painted porcelain head and reddish gold hair like his sister's. He slammed the doll on the floor, hard. Bettina screamed until he stopped. But the damage was done. Minnie's nose was chipped, her head cracked.

Seeing what had happened, his father raised his hand to smack the boy, then stopped. "Why are you so mean to your sister? She's done nothing to you!" While Bettina sobbed,

Father tried to repair the crack. "See, sweetie, she looks all right now," he said, handing the doll back. Bettina nodded but Werner could see she was still frightened. What might he break the next time his anger spilled out?

Werner took his sister's hand. "I won't be horrid again." She tried hard to smile.

For several days, however, his father barely spoke to him. He seemed deep in thought. Finally, he said, "I am going to take you to the orphanage, Werner. You will be safer there."

Werner stared at him, shocked. Leave their home? Go to an orphanage? How could his father do something so cruel?

"Not forever, my son," Father added, "just for now, I promise."

When they reached the orphanage, his father told Frau Schutz, "Ever since their mother died, life has been growing harder and harder. I feel that I can no longer keep Werner safe. Maybe if he's here with other boys, Jewish boys, and a kind woman...." His voice faded as he looked at Frau Schutz.

While they talked, Werner's head hung low. He stared at the dark, scratched, wooden floor. He had shamed his father and hurt his sister. No wonder he was being sent away from home.

The woman had doughy skin, brightened with rouge and lipstick. "I understand." She put an arm around Werner's shoulders. "Don't worry about your son. You do what you must do, that's how it is nowadays."

At last, Werner was leaving that dreary stone building. Running, then walking, then running again, he barely felt the chilly rain. Two miles into town and then through the town's streets, past the empty market square and the cathedral with its tall spire. He passed Jewish stores, now shut and boarded up, with big yellow stars painted crudely across the fronts. He didn't even notice; his mind was on one thing only – home.

Chapter Three

Hit by a strong gust of wind, Werner clutched his thin sweater and shivered. His heart pumped with excitement. Home. Home. Home. He didn't stop until he reached their small brown house with green shutters. He stared at the dark wooden door. Often, he had dreamed of running away and coming here on his own. But as long as he had felt unwanted, he didn't come. How he had longed for this one sweet moment! Home again, finally.

The door swung open as soon as he knocked. "Werner," Father murmured, hugging the boy warmly as soon as he stepped inside.

Gazing around the parlor, Werner's eyes feasted on stuff he knew well. A dumpy green sofa, the faded rose-covered carpet, dusty oil paintings, and a glass-fronted bookcase, overflowing with books. Everything seemed the same except…he spied an empty place on the floor in the parlor where his mother's shiny black piano once stood. Where had it gone?

"Werner!" Bettina ran up and hugged her brother, her face shining with delight. She held up her doll Minnie for him to kiss, and he gave the doll a big smack on its tiny pink porcelain lips. Bettina laughed aloud.

"You must be hungry," said Father. "I'll get you something to eat." He disappeared into the kitchen. Werner's heart swelled with pleasure. Finally he was back home where he belonged. He would be good now, cause no trouble and make his father proud. Whatever evils the family might endure – and they were many – they could face them together as a family.

For a long time, Father had tried to explain away the

troubles caused by the Nazis. "This is a difficult time for Germany. People have no work; they're hungry, desperate. They are blaming the Jews, as they always do when times are difficult."

That's what he said when he was fired from his job as a math teacher at a boys' school. That's what he said when they were forbidden to shop in stores owned by Christians. Or ride on the tram or sit in public parks. But when Jews began being hauled out of their houses and beaten up on the streets, or when they disappeared altogether, Father stopped making excuses. Now he sat home all day in a dark room listening to Beethoven and Brahms and Mendelssohn, the German music he so loved.

"Look what I have," exclaimed Father, rushing back in the room. "Black bread and a pot of herring!"

"*Wunderbar*, Papa!" Werner grinned. The herring smelled delicious, good and fishy.

"Bettina, set the table, will you?" The girl quickly laid out some dishes and silverware. Werner's family had never had a lot of things, yet they enjoyed what they had. Friday nights were special – a lace cloth spread on the table, china dishes, and a pair of silver candlesticks. Platters of meat and potatoes, rye bread, butter, and some sort of delicious cake.

"*Ja, ja,* very good." Father rubbed his hands, inspecting the black bread and herring as if it were a banquet.

"It is a very good day," Werner said. "A splendid day!"

"Here's a little treat." Father smiled, going to the cabinet and pulling out a bottle of *schnapps* and two little glasses. He poured the clear schnapps into each glass and handed one to his son. "Drink up."

Werner's eyes widened. Father had never offered him alcohol before. Taking a sip, the sharp liquor burned his throat, though he tried not to wince. Father watched carefully, his smile slowly fading. "You are probably wondering why I asked you to come?"

The boy shook his head. "This is our home where I belong. I knew you would ask me back, as soon as you could." He grinned as he held up the glass, ready for more. Bettina sidled up next to him like a kitten.

But his father's face had turned serious, almost stern. He put the bottle down hard on the table. "No, Werner, you must listen. I've got something very important." From a drawer he pulled out a thick envelope, opening it quickly. "For you, my son, only you."

He handed Werner a little booklet with a dark blue cover stamped with a Nazi swastika. Inside was a photo of a boy. The boy's cheeks were round, and his hair was combed neatly. Werner could barely recognize himself. It was an old photo, taken several years ago, when he was no more than nine.

"This is your passport," said Father. "You will never know what it took to get it." His eyes darted, however, toward the empty space where Mother's beautiful piano had stood. Was that the price of a passport? Werner wondered.

Father put the booklet back in the envelope and took out a large ticket. "Here's the *real* prize." He looked extremely pleased.

"What is it?" Werner asked, uncertain why he was being given this stuff.

"A ticket for the SS *Hansa*, leaving from Hamburg," he said. "You are a passenger."

"The *Hansa*? A ship?" Suddenly the boy's face became hot, his palms sweaty.

"It's going to America in three days," Father replied. "You'll find it on Pier 37."

"Me? Find a ship?" Werner exploded. "What are you saying? You mean for me to leave? Now? Why, I've just come home!"

Bettina's head jerked up. Father pursed his lips, saying nothing. That was his answer.

"No, Father, I'm not going." Werner quivered with rage.

"You can't make me go! You can't!"

His father stiffened, also angry. "You don't want to go? You don't know what you're saying!" He grabbed the boy's thin shoulders and started to shake him. But Werner pushed him away roughly. In that instant, the two realized they were equally strong.

"You don't want me here, do you?" Werner yelled. "You never wanted me here – that's why you put me in the orphanage. And now – now you're getting rid of me again!"

"No, Werner, that's not true," Father tried to explain, but the boy didn't let him. The pain of that long, lonely year jostled his heart.

"You don't care about me – you don't! You never have!"

Father looked frantic. "Werner, please, you don't understand. You must go. It's the best chance you have – to stay alive. That's what counts now. All that counts. Please, understand." His voice was so choked by now, he could say no more.

Werner stood staring at his father dumbly. He did understand. He'd seen it happen. The Nazi Gestapo pounding on a neighbor's door, hauling off grandparents, parents, even young children. They'd disappear. No one knew where. To escape that fate, many Jewish families had already fled the country. Others were desperately trying to find a place to go.

Werner's arm felt numb, almost lifeless, as he raised it slowly and reached for the envelope.

Yet immediately, lines of worry vanished from his father's face. "War has begun," he explained. "Soon no more ships will be traveling from Germany to America." His voice was now low and steady. "That's why you must leave right away."

"Why just me? What about you and Bettina?" Werner demanded. "Can't we all go together? We should go together!"

Father glanced at Bettina, his face sadder than his son had ever seen. "I wish it were possible. Truly, I do." He shook his head. "But I am too old and your sister is too young." He gathered Bettina in his arms and pressed her to his chest, stroking her fine hair. "We will stay together. Here, where we've always lived. During the good times and now the bad times."

Seeing the two of them so close hurt Werner yet again. They seemed like a complete family – without him.

Father must have read the look on Werner's face, for he pleaded once again. "You go first, son. Get a foothold in this new country – a place for us to live, a safe home." For a second his face glowed with hope. "Then we'll follow, I promise. We'll come too."

Was he telling the truth? Would they really come? Werner wondered….Yet his father wasn't giving him a choice. Either he went alone or none of them did. His father couldn't make him go, and yet he had to. Werner had to take the chance of going first, with the hope that Father and Bettina would follow. The other possibility – *no one going* – was like choosing a dead-end street. Nothing ahead, no way out.

Though Werner couldn't say no to his father's plea, he stalled. "How will I get to Hamburg? I've never been by myself. I don't know the way."

"The ship sails Wednesday. That gives you three days. It's too dangerous by train, so you'll need to walk, using road signs." He paused. "I know it is difficult, son. God knows, I wish I could go with you at least as far as Hamburg." He glanced at Bettina. "But being alone is better, because you can travel fast. And traveling fast is safer by far."

Father was speaking quickly now; he knew what he had to say. "I have written to a relative of your mother's named Esther. She will meet you on the pier when you arrive. She's promised to take care of you until…." He hesitated a moment…"until we can come." Then he went to a closet and pulled out a pair of boots, his own good hiking boots. "These are a bit too big, but better than what you've got."

He watched as Werner took off his shabby old shoes. Beneath them, his socks had more holes than yarn.

Bettina giggled. "Look at your toes."

Werner pulled off his socks and put on the boots. Though they didn't fit, he was pleased. His father had once belonged to a hiking club with stout Germans from town. He'd worn these boots proudly every weekend as they tromped through nearby forests. The boots smelled of better days.

Then his father fetched something else. "Here's a wool loden-cloth jacket that belonged to your mother," he said. "It's been packed in a trunk for years, so it doesn't have a yellow star sewn on it."

The two stared at the coat and not at each other. Both knew the risk of not wearing a star. The Nazi government required every Jew to sew a big yellow star onto all their clothes. To be caught without one meant jail or worse. But wearing a star was also dangerous, because it drew attention. Werner could be stopped by anyone and beaten up or even killed.

He put on the pale blue jacket, the color of the sky on a spring morning. The wool carried the faint scent of mothballs, yet its warmth surrounded him like his mother's embrace. Oh, how he missed *Mutti*! She had died four years ago of a fever when he was eight and Bettina was only three. In a few days, she went from being a charming lively woman to being so weak that she couldn't lift her head from the pillow. She barely recognized Werner and Bettina as the children pressed the bed, weeping. In the last instant of her life, however, she grasped her son's hand tightly. "*Werner, mein Liebling, mach es gut, es wird alles gut werden.*" Take care, everything will be all right. That's what she had thought. But then, Werner figured, she had died before things got really bad.

Still, he was glad that she wasn't there for this terrible day. How could he have said good-bye to her? And would she have been able to send him off to such an uncertain future? Putting on his mother's coat, he slid his hands into the pockets. His fingers closed around a tight wad of money that he pulled out.

Father shrugged. "A few Reichsmarks. All I could manage."

The big old clock in the hall began chiming. His father's face suddenly looked grey and tired. "You must get going, Werner. You need a good start before nightfall." He carefully put the envelope with the ticket and passport in the boy's knapsack. "Use your head, Werner. Don't speak to anyone unless you have to."

Now there was no reason to delay, but Werner's feet felt rooted to the old carpet. He gazed at Bettina and Father, wanting to hold fast to everything he knew and loved. He had been home less than an hour and already he was leaving – with no idea when he might return, or when he might see them again.

He started to say, "No, no. I can't, I can't...."

But suddenly, Bettina rushed over and flung her thin arms around her brother. He grabbed hold of her and kissed the top of her head. Since the death of *Mutti*, Bettina had been the sweet, soft part of their lives. For a moment her delicate fingers clung to his shirt. Then Bettina let go and ran to the window.

"Go, Werner, go quickly," she called, turning her face to the cool glass pane like they were playing a game.

Father led him to the door and pointed north. "Hamburg's that way. You'll find signs on the edge of town." He gazed at his son hard for a moment, as if sealing his face in the vault of his memory. He put his hand on the boy's shoulder. "I have one minute to give you a lifetime of advice, and… and I can think of nothing to say." Then he squeezed his son's shoulder until it hurt. "Only this, Werner…wherever you go, remember how much your mother and I loved each other. And loved you, our children."

"But you will come," Werner insisted, his voice shaking. "You said you would."

"Write to us, Werner, as soon as you arrive," Father's eyes grew bright. "Tell us all about this new country. Everything. We so look forward to getting your letters. Please write."

A moment later, the door swung shut. Rain pelted Werner's face, falling much harder than before. Father and Bettina were inside. He was outside. Through the window, he saw Bettina waving and waving. As if he were simply going to the market as he once did and would return soon with sweets in his pocket.

Werner slowly turned and walked away, glancing back once or twice. His face and hair were quickly drenched by the rain. The air seemed much colder, too. He pulled his mother's jacket close around him. Its warmth was all that remained of home.

Chapter Four

After the young man, Gunther, left his side, Werner kept walking toward Hamburg. Soon, he lost count of the kilometers. The sky grew as dark as the road. The rain had let up but the wind still blew hard. His heavy boots, now coated with mud, seemed to grow heavier and heavier. Fortunately, a farmer pulling a big rick of hay slowed his pair of draft-horses. "Wanna rest your soles a bit?" he called out and Werner eagerly climbed on.

He fell asleep on the wagon, not waking until dawn the next day when a loud rooster crowed in his ear. The sky was clear, and he figured he only had 25 kilometers remaining on his journey.

Toward the end of the day, however, he lost his way. There were no signs – just wide empty fields and little cottages. He passed a few folks but was afraid to ask directions. Finally, he saw a plump child playing in the little fenced yard of a stone cottage. She looked about six; her hair was so fair and fluffy, it shone almost pink in the sunlight. She was commanding a shaggy brown dog to jump up and grab a piece of bread.

"*Wunderbar*, Reiner, wonderful!" She rewarded Reiner with another piece.

Werner's stomach growled at the sight of bread. Did he dare ask her for a bit? Seeing him pause at the gate, the child stared and then cried out, "*Mutti, Mutti!*"

Immediately, a blonde young woman hurried out the door. "What is it, Lottie, *Liebling*?" Seeing Werner, she stopped and stared too. In a trembling voice, he asked, "Do you know the way to Hamburg?"

The child's mother shrugged. "Cut through the fields over there; you'll get there in a day."

One day. That's all the time he had left.

"*Danke!*" Werner yelled and started in that direction, but the woman called after him. "*Warte eine Minute.*" Wait a minute. She ran in the house and brought back a big soft roll, warm from the oven.

"Here, Lottie, my sweet, give this to the poor boy." Lottie shyly brought the roll to him.

Werner wolfed it down, muttering thanks. Lottie's pale blue eyes grew wide. "*Gott segne Sie,*" she murmured. God bless you. Then she ran back to her mother and the two watched as he stumbled across a wide field plowed in long muddy furrows.

The roll from Lottie kept him going. Soon he reached a road sign: *Hamburg, 23 km.* I can make it...I *will* make it, thought Werner.

But just as he began feeling good, a truck filled with soldiers pulled up. Three or four young men in Nazi SS uniforms climbed out. The way they yelled at one another and staggered along the road, Werner guessed they were drunk. He ducked his head, hoping they wouldn't notice him, and began walking faster. That was a mistake.

"*Dummer Junge!*" one shouted. Stupid boy! And the soldier began chasing Werner. His feet in the big boots were already blistered. The road was so muddy, he slipped several times. The soldier came so close he could smell sour beer on his breath. Fingers grabbed at his hair. Just before seizing Werner, however, the fellow slipped, falling flat in a mud puddle.

"You silly clown," his friends called out and stopped to pull him up. Werner kept running, as fast as possible, and no one followed.

Far down the road, he finally stopped, his lungs aching. His teeth were clamped shut. There was a damp patch on his pants where he'd peed. And his hands still trembled. What if the soldier had grabbed me? Werner thought. What then? A pistol shot to his head, his body thrown in the bushes. Things like that happened, he'd heard. No one would ever know – not his father or the lady waiting for him in America.

Werner could barely walk another twenty minutes. His body ached; every muscle was stiff. Finally, however, he found a little shed. Jerking open the wooden door, he collapsed on the soggy hay next to two sheep and three lambs. He curled up next to the five woolly beasts and breathed in their dank warm smell. Bits of hay stuck to his hair and jacket, but he knew the animals didn't care how he looked.

He tried to ignore the groan in his stomach. Even thin soup from the orphanage would have tasted good that night. Yet how proud Father would be that he had made it so far.

Chapter Five

Hamburg, at last. Rows of red-brick buildings, narrow streets, churches soaring skyward, dozens of shops. Years ago, Werner had come to the city with his family. He had gazed eagerly at the automobiles, stores, and crowds of people. His hand had rested securely in *Mutti's* hand....

Now, huge red banners with black swastikas were draped across every building. Nazi soldiers with hefty guns stood on nearly every corner. As he passed, one soldier eyed him sharply and shouted, "Where are you going?"

Werner froze. "I...I'm going to my grandmother's house."

The soldier's eyes narrowed, his grip on his gun tightened. "What about school? Today's a school day, isn't it?"

What day was it? Sunday, Monday, Wednesday? Werner's mind went blank. "A school day, yes," he stammered. "But... but Grandma is sick. I must go and see her."

The soldier grunted and waved him on with his gun. Werner walked quickly. Time was running out. Three days had passed. Where was the SS *Hansa*? What if he missed it? How could he return to Father and say he had failed?

Fortunately, at that moment, he caught a strong whiff of sea – a sharp, salty odor. In a few minutes, his nose led him to the pier. One giant ship after another was lined up, with scores of dockworkers loading cargo.

"Where is Pier 37?" He asked an old guy with a scraggly grey beard, leaning on a barrel. "Whatcha want to know for?" the man replied. "You ain't going nowhere yourself, are you?"

Werner shrugged. "No particular reason. Just heard it's a great ship to see."

The old man scratched his skimpy beard and pointed down the wharf. "Thar's the *Hansa*; it ain't far."

Minutes later, Werner stood gazing up at the ship. The *Hansa* stretched up three stories and seemed a city block long. Like Noah's Ark, it seemed the vessel could hold all the pairs of creatures God wanted to save. Only now, there were people, hundreds and hundreds, seeking safety.

All around him men and women were hugging, kissing, and crying – both the ones leaving and the ones left behind. Werner longed to see a friendly face, someone saying good-bye to him. For a moment, he pretended a slight man blowing his nose into a white handkerchief was Father. A little girl squeezing a doll was Bettina. But it wasn't true. He was alone, totally alone.

That was the moment he first saw her. A slender girl, ten or eleven, dressed all in purple. A purple wool coat trimmed in black fur, purple leggings, and a little purple cap topped by a black furry ball. Her fragile heart-shaped face was framed in thick dark curls. With pale skin and startling dark eyes, she was the most perfect-looking girl he had ever seen. Except she was crying. Tears soaked her cheeks and dripped from her chin.

The girl clung to a tall handsome man in a heavy dark wool coat. He looked like a wealthy lawyer or banker. The girl clung to him like a young monkey, afraid of falling from a tree. "*Mein Vater,*" she cried again and again. My father.

The tall man tried to comfort his daughter. "Anika, darling little Anika, *mein Schatz.*" He knelt down and hugged her. "I will follow soon. Don't worry, my darling little girl, you will see me in America very soon."

Why, those were the very words that his father had said to him! That he would follow, that he'd come soon to America. Was it true? Would this wealthy gentleman and his father both come?

Of course Father will come, thought Werner. If I do what I need to do – go first and get a foothold in the new country and then write and let them know they'll be safe. Then, surely, Bettina and Father will follow. Werner quickly turned and almost ran up the gangplank.

Only halfway up, however, a giant ugly man in a sailor's uniform blocked Werner's path. The sailor had a flat round face with a squashed nose, like it had been punched too many times. *"Du Schnottnase! Du Dreckstück!"* He gave Werner a rough push. "Where do you think you're going, you snotty-faced dirtbag! Trying to sneak past me!"

Werner pulled out his ticket and tried to stick it in the man's face. But the sailor ignored the papers and starting pushing him back down the gangplank. "Who do you think you are? I see by your dirty clothes you are no better than me. You won't get on board. You can't get past me."

But just as Werner was about to end up back on the pier, he felt someone's hand on his shoulder. Glancing back, he saw Anika's father. The tall gentleman faced the sailor squarely. "What's going on here? Why did you stop this boy from boarding the ship?"

The sailor scowled, then glanced at Werner. "He's a nobody, sir. Look at his clothes, his dirty fingernails. Don't waste your time on him. He wants to sneak onboard like a million other nobodies. Thinks he can go to America, land of the free." The sailor jerked his head to one side and spit scornfully into the water below.

In that instant, Werner handed his ticket and passport to the gentleman, who looked at both carefully. "Werner Berlinger? Is that you?" Werner nodded, knowing his thin grimy face didn't resemble the little boy in the picture. But the girl's father was convinced. He turned again to the sailor, his voice loud and firm. "This boy has passage on this ship. Who are you, a dumb sailor, to stop him? Let him on board this minute or I'll call the Captain."

"Yes, sir, of course, sir." The sailor muttered, glaring at Werner. "Why didn't you show me your ticket, boy?" Then he stepped aside, letting Werner board the ship. The gentleman nodded curtly, then returned to his daughter on the pier. The moment he was gone, the sailor stuck his face close to Werner's. "You know what this ticket says?"

The boy shook his head.

"You're below deck, third tier, not much higher than us seamen," he snickered. "And don't forget it. Don't dare try sneaking up with the rich folks where you don't belong, you hear?"

Werner nodded. By now he was eager to get off the deck and find his lowly compartment. Yet he lingered another moment, glancing back at Anika. He saw the girl give her father a final kiss, wipe her eyes with a tiny lace handkerchief, and stuff the hankie in the pocket of her purple coat. Then, with head erect, she walked toward the ship. At her side, a thin young woman with frizzy blonde hair and a sharp nose clutched at a batch of whimpering children. As the sad group reached the ship, their parents on the pier grasped hands and leaned on one another, forming a knot of grief and hope. Just like his father, Werner thought, their dreams for the future were traveling ahead of them.

Stumbling down the ship's narrow steps, he finally found the cabin listed on his ticket. Just as the sailor had said, it was near the bottom. Pulling open a metal door, he spied a tiny cubicle with barely room for one. A shelf with a thin mattress served as a bed at night and a seat during the day. There was a tin basin with a mirror above it, though the glass was so old and blotchy, Werner could barely see himself.

For a moment, he stared at himself. With grey eyes and thick sandy hair, he was a mix of his fair mother and dark-haired father. But years of bad food, worry, and just plain tiredness all showed. Yellowish skin stretched tight across gaunt cheekbones. His eyes were dull, yet a flicker of light now showed in them. He had done what Father had asked: made it to Hamburg, made it to the ship *Hansa*.

Werner turned away from the mirror. Even for a scrawny twelve-year-old, the room was a tight fit. Still, it was all his! And it was warm. Steaming hot, in fact, as the engines for the ship ground away on the other side of a thin wall. The ship's furnace was close by as well.

Latching the narrow door, Werner allowed the warmth to flood his chilled muscles. He untied the boots, carefully removed them, and pushed the pair under the shelf. He slowly rinsed the bloody blisters on his feet with warm water from the sink. Coarse sheets, clean but stained from long use, were stacked on the mattress. There was no pillow or blanket but no need for either. Werner rolled up his mother's jacket and stuck it under his head. I'll nap a short while, he figured. But his body had other ideas. After days of walking and running, being uncertain and afraid, his eyes shut and stayed shut. He slept, snug as a rabbit in its fur-lined hole after being chased by hungry foxes.

Chapter Six

Time feels different on a ship crossing the ocean than it does on land.

When Werner awoke at last, he lay still for several moments. How long had he slept? One day, two days? Was it night? Was it day?

His body remembered the journey from home to Hamburg and refused, at first, to stir. Finally, however, curiosity drew him out of the snug cabin. The ship was like a city afloat. What might he find on board? Jerking open the door, he stepped into a narrow corridor crowded with people. There were several families traveling on the ship's lowest level, like him. The clothes on the older people were black, their faces thin and haggard.

A child almost crashed into him. The little boy was playing chase with two other youngsters. For them, the ship was a giant playground. They were sneaking in and out of doors, hiding behind trunks and baggage, giggling and teasing one another. Werner watched for a moment, enviously. He hadn't played with such a sense of fun and freedom for years. When a little girl with coppery curls dashed past, Werner grabbed the child and began to tickle her. She looked up with a startled face.

"Sorry," murmured Werner, red-faced, and he quickly released her.

A tough old woman, dressed in black from headscarf to shoes, was seated on a trunk at the edge of the hallway. She gnawed on a chunk of hard bread; a fat salami stuck out of a bag slung over her shoulder. Werner's stomach growled fiercely at the pungent odor, but he didn't dare ask.

Eyeing him, the old woman sighed loudly. "We're blessed to leave that evil place." She jerked her head in the direction she supposed was Germany. "My oldest son was arrested months ago. No word of him since. My youngest headed south with several friends. I pray to God he made it to Palestine." The old woman glanced upward. She spoke in Yiddish, a language many Jews spoke. Werner could understand Yiddish, though his educated father had always insisted that his family speak only German. "As for my poor sister," said the woman, pulling out a large dirty handkerchief and blowing her nose, "she wasn't well enough to make the trip. God alone must protect her now."

Werner nodded a bit impatiently. He'd heard enough sad stories for the present, and was eager to stretch his limbs and explore the ship. Muttering an excuse, he headed down the corridor. First, he clambered up one set of rungs and then another. Finally he reached the highest deck and pushed hard on the door. Outside the wind was blowing so fiercely, he had to lean against it with all his weight. At last, the door opened a few inches and he squeezed out, stepping into the blackest night he'd ever seen. Above, the sky was dark as coal, below, swelled inky waves. The deck was empty. There was no moon nor any trace of land.

It was as if Germany – the only home Werner had known, where he'd learned to walk and talk, played with friends and fought with foes, where his dear *Mutti* had kissed him for the last time – that land was *gone*, erased from the map.

Werner peered down at the somber waves below. What lay beneath? Sharks and sea monsters and the wrecks of long forgotten ships. He gripped the rail and leaned forward, a sharp icy wind smacking his face. His eyes watered and he pulled his mother's jacket close around his chest. It felt like her arms hugging him tight.

Being forced to leave home, Werner knew, was nothing new. History books are filled with stories of people who must leave one country and go to another. Disease, hunger, war, poverty – those are some of the reasons people go – ending one story and beginning another. People often leave with a shadow of unhappiness in their hearts and their eyes bright with dreams. Indeed, for Werner, one nightmare was over, yet he had no idea what lay ahead....

He tried to imagine the United States. But the only pictures in his head were what he'd seen in movies: cowboys and Indians, cops and gangsters. Was America really like that? Gunfights in the streets, bandits robbing banks, and wildly painted savages on horseback? Or was America the land of the free, as Father often said? A haven for all people of every race and religion? What did that mean? What did it *feel* like? Soon he would find out. He'd know for himself what the United States of America was truly like.

His stomach gurgled loudly and he swayed dizzily. A day or two had passed since he'd had even a scrap of food. Afraid he might slip off the deck and become a shark's dinner, Werner turned and pulled open the ship's door. There must be plenty of food somewhere on the ship, but where?

Fortunately, Werner was used to sneaking around in search of food. He crept through the corridors, sniffing every which way, like a rat. He stalked the narrow hallways, peeking in doors, passing libraries, ballrooms, and game rooms, but no food. Then suddenly, as he turned a corner, a delicious aroma hit his nostrils. What could it be? A beef brisket, leg of lamb, or a goose roasting in an oven? A few steps further and Werner spied wide double doors. Behind them, loud laughter mingled with the clatter of pots and pans.

Carefully slipping through the doors, Werner snuck behind some shelves. The large kitchen bustled with cooks, working nonstop. They laughed and joked loudly with one another. Gazing round, Werner saw that every inch in the large room was covered with food – platters of meat, fish, loaves of bread, vegetables, potatoes, cakes, and tarts. A veritable feast from

Heaven! His stomach twisted painfully from the delicious aroma. He was starving! Yet how would he steal even one bite from this bountiful display of food?

A minute later he saw his chance, as a plump, pretty woman with blonde pigtails put a dish of roast lamb on a nearby table and walked away.

Crouching low, Werner crept closer and closer until he was right beneath the table. Then he carefully stuck up some fingers, pulled off a tiny piece and stuck it in his mouth. Nothing had ever tasted so good! He reached again and again and again – until, all of a sudden, he felt his arm seized in an iron grip.

"Mein Gott, dieser kleine Schlingel!" You little rascal! yelled the blonde cook. She turned triumphantly to her fellow workers. "Look at this guy, eating all my good roast lamb. Gobbling it up as fast as I cook it!"

She dragged the boy to the center of the room. The din in the kitchen ceased as the cooks stopped and stared right at him. Still gripping Werner's arm, the woman seized a huge butcher knife with her other hand, holding it close to his nose. He shut his eyes tight, praying death would come quickly. Still alive a few seconds later, however, he opened his eyes a slit. The cook was whacking off pieces of juicy pink meat from the roast, then piling them on a plate.

"Here you go, skinny lad." She thrust the plate at him. "My name is Elsa. You remind me of my six brothers back home in Düsseldorf. Always hungry!"

With the dish in his lap, Werner began eating and eating and then eating some more. His stomach ballooned, then it started to ache, but still he pushed in more and more food. This is paradise, he thought. If only my hungry friends Mandel, Victor, Sammel, and Lutz were here to share. What a wondrous feast we would have!

A moment later, however, his bliss was shattered by a familiar voice. "Where's my darling Elsa?"

Glancing up, Werner saw the big ugly sailor who'd tried

to push him off the ship. The guy didn't look in his direction, however. He strode across the room heading straight for Elsa, who was now rolling out pie dough on a marble slab. When he reached her side, the pretty, plump woman giggled and planted a wet kiss on his lips. That made the sailor so happy, he wrapped his thick arms around her.

Werner was just starting to relax when Elsa pointed toward him. "Look, Eckhard, sweetie, at the skinny little guy I'm feeding!"

Glancing at Werner, the sailor's big smile turned into a scowl. "That thieving scoundrel!" he yelled. "He doesn't belong here! Not in the first-class kitchen with all the best food."

Werner leaped up, letting his plate of food crash to the floor. Dashing for the doors, he very nearly escaped. But, at the last second, the sailor grabbed his shirt and spun him around, his angry eyes inches from the boy's, his fist raised to sock him in the jaw.

"Eckhard, darling, don't pick on that poor child," Elsa called out. "See how miserable he is?" Her words caused the sailor to pause an instant, just long enough for Werner to jerk out of his grasp and scramble out the door.

Chapter Seven

If only he could find the way to his little cabin. Dashing down one hallway after another, Werner searched for the steps to the lower level. Behind, he could hear footsteps thunder after him. Doors lined the corridor on either side, but like in a nightmare, every door was shut tight.

Suddenly, a door cracked open and a girl peeked out. She had dark, curly hair and dark eyes. Werner recognized her at once – Anika, the girl who had been weeping on the pier. The two stared at one another a second, then she gestured, "Would you like to come in?"

For a second, Werner didn't budge. How could he enter this strange girl's room? Then, a heavy footstep sounded down the corridor and he quickly ducked inside. Anika shut the door and fastened it. Werner's heart was pounding – both from running and from something else – the feeling he got from being near this girl.

"Your name is Werner, isn't it?" she murmured. "I heard Father say it."

He nodded. "Werner Berlinger."

"My name is Anika. Anika Frankenthaler." A tiny smile crossed her lips. She was wearing a soft, fluffy white sweater and a dark green velvet skirt. Around her neck was a string of shiny white pearls; in each ear a matching pearl glowed.

Anika's stateroom was ten times bigger than Werner's compartment. The bed was covered with a silky bedspread. A gold-framed mirror hung over the large white sink. There was a thick rug on the floor, and a lamp, big as a chandelier, hung on the ceiling. Clothes were piled high on a chair. It looked as if

Anika had pulled everything out of her trunk without bothering to hang anything up.

At a glance, he could see the clothes were new and costly, not old and worn like his. Werner stiffened, feeling awkward and shy. His father was a teacher; their friends had been other teachers, government clerks, or simple shopkeepers. He wasn't used to being around wealthy people, people who owned large houses with servants and had fancy chauffeur-driven automobiles.

Also, the past year in the orphanage, he knew, had roughened his words and manners. He wasn't sure how to talk and behave with this young lady. And he certainly didn't want to appear foolish.

Anika watched him quietly. "Would you please stay with me a while?" she asked. "I find it rather dull and boring on this ship." A shadow crossed her fragile face, then her eyes quickly brightened. "Perhaps you'd like something to eat? I have fruit and candy."

Though stuffed to bursting, Werner nodded. It had been such a long time since he'd seen either fruit or candy.

From under the bed, Anika pulled out a large candy box, trimmed with a wide, green satin ribbon. Inside were rows of luscious chocolates wrapped in gold and silver foil. Werner carefully chose one, removed its gleaming foil, and popped it in his mouth. A cherry dripping in creamy sweetness! The candy didn't sit well, however, on top of his stuffed belly. Werner covered his mouth to stifle a loud belch.

Anika giggled. "My goodness, you aren't sick, are you?"

He frowned, shaking his head and reaching for another chocolate. "Of course not. I'm just fine."

Her lips curled into a little pout. "I hate this ship, don't you? I didn't want to leave Germany. Father forced me to go."

"So where is your mother?" Werner glanced around. "Why didn't she come with you?"

Anika's smile faded, her lower lip trembled, and a tear

welled up in one eye. "I…I haven't any mother now…" Her gaze dropped and the tear slid down her cheek.

The two of us do have something in common, Werner thought. We are both *motherless*. He gazed at the many beautiful things in the stateroom. Does any of this stuff matter if you don't have a dear *Mutter* to hug and kiss you, to sing lullabies and say how much she loves you?

Spying a book spread open on the bed, Werner noted that the words weren't in German. He picked it up, "What is this?"

"I'm learning English," Anika said, wiping away the tear. "I speak French already," she smiled a gave a little curtsey. "*Je suis une tres jolie fille, n'est-ce pas?*" She smiled mischievously. "You do think I'm pretty, don't you?"

Werner pursed his lips and felt his face flush, but didn't say what he thought: *Yes, you are pretty, but you are also very spoiled.*

Anika didn't seem to notice and kept talking. "My family traveled a lot before the wicked Nazis came and took everything. Our house and furniture and paintings and books." She took the book from his hands. "We kept just a few things like this splendid *Alice and Wonderland*. Do you know it?"

Werner shook his head, thinking how stupid he must seem to this girl.

She opened the book and read aloud: "*You are old, Father William, the Young Man said…and yet you incessantly stand on your head—do you think at your age it is right?*"

Looking up, laughter poured from her lips like sunlight. Though he didn't understand the words, Werner was delighted to see her laugh so freely.

"But are you alone on this ship?" he asked.

"Of course not. How could I travel by myself? I'm only eleven," she snapped. "I'm with Miss Feldenbaum. She's accompanying sixteen children to the United States." She looked annoyed. "Miss Feldenbaum is very sweet, but I don't want to go to America. I've heard it has terrible food and no fashionable dresses."

Terrible food and no fashionable dresses? Werner couldn't listen to another word.

"Now you're being silly," he exclaimed. "You know we don't have a choice, either of us. We had to leave Germany because of the damn Nazis. And I'm not sorry, not any more. I wish every Jew could get out. Every Jew!" As he spoke, his hands clenched into fists.

Anika's eyes widened. She was clearly surprised by Werner's loud voice and strong words. He was surprised, too. As long as he could remember, Father had said, "Whatever happens, don't ever show your feelings, Werner." And so he had kept his feelings neatly tucked behind a blank mask until that moment. So why had he burst out now? Did he feel freer on the ship, moving swiftly away from Germany? Or had this girl somehow pried him open like a clam in warm ocean water?

Whatever the reason, Anika now spoke quietly. "I can see you haven't had a very nice time of it, either."

Werner slid his fists into the pockets of his blue jacket and hunched over a bit. He recalled the boys forcing the chalk into his hand and the Nazi soldier grabbing at his hair before slipping on the mud. "No, I haven't."

She observed him carefully, "Why are you wearing that coat in here? It's very warm. You should take it off."

"I'd rather keep it on," he muttered. Though his coat had less scent now, he could still catch a whiff of *Mutti*, of home.

"Suit yourself." Anika shrugged, then walked across the room. Her dainty bare feet sank into the carpet. Werner longed to remove his boots and feel the soft rug on his own sore toes, but he didn't dare. What would this well-bred girl think of his red, bruised skin and puffy blisters?!

Anika pointed to a card table with cards spread out for a game of solitaire. "What games do you know?"

"*Skat* and *Schafkopf,*" Werner quickly replied. These were popular games known by any German child.

"Good," Anika announced. "Let's play together." She sat

down, picked up the deck and began shuffling deftly.

The two played again and again for nearly an hour. Because she was a girl, Werner figured he could beat her easily, like when he had played checkers with his sister. Often he had let Bettina win to keep her happy, but there was no need to let Anika win. She was a sharp card player, grinning triumphantly whenever she put down a winning card.

Finally, however, Anika yawned and stared at her gold wristwatch. "It's very late, almost dawn. We'll hear the breakfast gong soon."

"Breakfast gong?" Werner perked up, his stomach no longer feeling so stuffed.

"When the gong sounds in the dining room, Miss Feldenbaum fetches us. We eat together at a long table." She yawned again, barely bothering to cover her mouth.

"Can *anyone* eat in the dining room? Or do you need money?" Werner asked.

"Silly boy, of course you get meals with your ship's ticket." Her glance took in his clothes and boots. "Though maybe you don't eat in the first-class dining room where we eat."

By now Anika's eyelids were drooping over her dark eyes, and she sank down on the bed.

In a few seconds, Werner had slipped out the door and he soon found his way back to his little cabin. Lying down on the hard narrow shelf, he stared up at the ceiling. Damp with moisture and heat from the engine room, the dull greenish paint overhead had begun to peel.

A ship is an odd place, Werner thought. All sorts of people are thrown together – people whose paths would otherwise never cross. Yet, as different as he and Anika were, their stories were similar. They had the same worries and fears; they shared the same hope. He was certain that both of them wanted most of all to be with their families in a safe place. And soon they would be. He pictured it clearly in his mind – Father, Bettina, and he – all together in a new home, perhaps a house with a garden and room for a shaggy brown dog. He had always wanted a dog, or any sort of pet.

Rolling over on his side, with *Mutti's* coat tucked under his head, Werner closed his eyes. Better not to think too much, just let the rocking motion of the waves lull him to sleep, a deep sleep with no dreams and no nightmares.

Chapter Eight

10 September, 1939

Dear Father,

I have found writing paper on board the ship. And they have a little post box where I can drop the letter and they promise to mail it. I wish to report on everything that has happened since I left home. First of all, I'm sure you were worried. But I want to assure you that I made the trip from home to Hamburg with no problems. It was a very easy trip. Then I boarded the ship without difficulty. Everyone has been nice and helpful to me. Today we are somewhere on the Atlantic Ocean, though I'm not sure where. They won't tell us. I just know we're lucky there are no storms. The waves have been smooth and hardly anyone is seasick.

Life on board is perfect. It took me a short while to find the third class dining room, but now I eat there every day. Tonight we had potato soup, boiled chicken and peas and cabbage, with pudding for dessert. And you can eat as much as you like. Imagine that!! I eat so much that people at my table laugh.

I have met a really special girl named Anika. We play cards together almost every night. Or she reads to me from her English book, "Alice in Wonderland." Do you know it? Though I don't understand the words, it's fun to listen. And just think, Father — soon I'll be speaking and reading in English too.

The only thing missing is you and Bettina. How I long to see both of you. Every night I pray that you will follow on the very next ship leaving Hamburg.

Please give my sister many hugs and kisses.
Your son, Werner

Whenever Werner and Anika played cards, the giant candy box stayed open. Once they had demolished the top layer of candy, Werner had been surprised to find a layer beneath it, and another beneath that, too.

One evening, Anika looked rather bored. "Do you know where we are?" she asked.

Werner shrugged. "In the middle of the ocean somewhere." He reached for a chocolate and put it in his mouth.

"Yes, the Captain says we will arrive in three days," she said, "if the ship isn't bombed or hit by torpedoes."

"Torpedoes?" Werner nearly gagged. "But this is a passenger ship. And...and Germany and the United States are not at war."

"True. It would be a mistake." Anika carefully laid a card down on the table. "But mistakes like that do happen."

The piece of chocolate stuck in Werner's throat.

"And do you know what will happen if we are bombed?" Anika looked almost gleeful.

Werner thought of the millions of sharks in the ocean.

40

"There are lifeboats," he declared. "I've seen them on deck."

"You think there's room for every passenger in those lifeboats? Remember the Titanic?" Anika giggled and reached for a gold-wrapped piece of candy. The notion of becoming shark's food didn't appear to ruin her appetite.

Werner glanced at Anika. She was waiting for him to play a card. He couldn't decide which one to put down. He had never before had a friend who was a girl. It was mostly pleasant but often felt somewhat wobbly, like sitting on a chair with one short leg.

Two days later, Werner happened to see Anika in the hallway. The dinner gong had sounded in the first-class dining room. Miss Feldenbaum was leading her group of sixteen. The children were clean and neat, but not so well behaved. They pushed, pinched, and teased one another. The thin young woman seemed very weary of keeping order.

Werner started to greet Anika, but before he'd said a word, Miss Feldenbaum spied him. She quickly surveyed his shabby clothes and oversized boots, then pulled Anika aside and whispered to her. Anika glanced at Werner with a weak smile, then turned and walked away with the others.

He pretended not to notice and hurried in the other direction. After all, why should a girl like Anika pay attention to him? She'd grown up with nannies and governesses, with French tutors and music lessons. Why, it was likely that she'd only spent time with him because they were together on the ship. On a forced journey that neither of them wanted. They would soon go their separate ways. Never to meet again.

Indeed, the next morning, the ship reached New York harbor. After weeks of travel across an empty ocean, they were surrounded by other ocean liners, fishing boats, tugs and barges. A clamor of whistles and horns and bells filled the air. In the midst of the harbor loomed the statue of a giant lady holding a lamp high in the air. Everyone rushed onto deck and shouted,

"The Statue of Liberty! The Statue of Liberty!"

"Ain't that the most beautiful sight you ever saw?" said the old woman dressed in black, her cheeks wet with tears. She and other immigrants left the ship at Ellis Island to be inspected before entering the country. But since Werner had a visitor's visa, he remained on board to disembark with the other passengers.

Pressed against the rail, Werner gazed at the huge city. Tall buildings shot up, one right after the other. The buildings were taller than the highest castle tower or cathedral spire in Germany. There were far too many to count, all stretching skyward.

The minute the ship tied up to the pier, people began jostling and pushing and crowding down the gangplank. A gruff American official looked quickly at his documents, signed a form and waved him on.

Instead of heading off the ship, however, he squeezed back on board. All morning his stomach had been tossed by a jumble of emotions – excitement, worry, joy, and sadness. Leaving the ship meant taking one more step away from everything he knew – away from Father and Bettina and toward an unknown future. Already he could hear the jabber of that strange language, English. Though he yearned to understand, he couldn't make out the meaning of a single word.

Father had said that a lady would meet him on the pier. But he hadn't said what she would look like. Or how she would find Werner in the crowd. He decided to climb to the deck high above and watch others depart. In their hurry, no one seemed to notice. From his safe perch, he scanned the people on the pier, hoping to see someone searching for him. Dozens of people greeted one another, but no one appeared to be looking for a boy like him.

Werner watched as the big cargo doors on the side of the ship slid open. Shiny Mercedes Benz limousines rolled out, thoroughbred horses pranced off, and a dozen cages of loudly barking dogs, German Shepherds and Doberman Pinschers, left the ship.

Then he saw Miss Feldenbaum emerge on the first-class gangplank leading her little posse of children.

Spying Anika, Werner couldn't help calling out. She was dressed in the purple outfit she'd worn the first day he had seen her. Her black shining curls were neatly combed beneath the purple hat. She wore gloves and carried a black fur muff. As usual, her head was high, her gaze confident. Hearing her name, Anika's head whirled around. Her eyes searched for him.

Werner waved wildly. Glimpsing him, she started to wave back. But at that moment Miss Feldenbaum took her arm and urged her down the gangplank. Anika continued walking and didn't look back again.

Frowning, Werner now wished he'd had a chance to say good-bye. Anika was a bit spoiled and pampered, but she was a fun, lively girl. He would miss her.

As soon as Miss Feldenbaum's group reached the pier, people surged forth to claim various children. An old white-haired couple, a young couple, a lady in a spiffy suit and hat all seemed eager to meet their new charges. Soon every child was accounted for, except Anika. She sat on the edge of her trunk, trying to appear calm and dignified. Every time a car passed, however, she peered anxiously in its direction. Miss Feldenbaum paced up and down, glancing from time to time at her watch.

The minutes ticked by. Ten minutes. Twenty minutes. Thirty minutes. Anika looked more and more desperate. *I'd better go down and cheer her up*, thought Werner. He started to move, but at that moment a shiny limousine pulled up. A chauffeur in a fancy black uniform climbed out and spoke to Miss Feldenbaum. Clearly relieved, she pointed to Anika. The chauffeur picked up the girl's luggage and put it in the car's trunk. Then he held open the door and Anika disappeared within.

As the limousine pulled away, Werner whispered softly, "*Auf Wiedersehen, Anika.*" Goodbye. He felt sure she'd do well with her new American family. They probably lived in a grand house with plenty of servants – like her home in Germany before the Nazis arrived and stole everything!

Still, Werner wondered why Anika's host family didn't come to greet her themselves. Why did they just send the chauffeur, and he wasn't even on time. Werner considered for a moment. Ah yes, the family was probably planning a big welcome party for Anika with cake, fruit punch, and ice cream. That's why they didn't come! She'd do fine with them, of course she would. A girl with her charm always does well.

Werner lingered on the upper deck for a few more minutes. The ship was now very quiet. It seemed as if the seamen, the cooks, the ship's captain, everyone had gone. The pier appeared deserted as well. He could see that no one was looking for him. What would he do in this giant city without a place to live or food to eat? Perhaps he should remain on board. Soon the cooks would return and start filling the kitchen with their laughter and bountiful food. His warm little compartment beckoned....

Yet Werner knew he couldn't stay where he was. What would his father say if he hadn't done what he'd been asked to do? If he didn't get a foothold in this new country? If he didn't write and describe his new life so Father and Bettina would come? He was clever and strong. He could figure out something, some way to survive.

Climbing down from the upper deck, Werner headed straight for the gangplank. But just as he reached it, a hand seized his jacket, jerking him off his feet. Ekhard's loud voice sounded in his ear. "Ya little scoundrel! On yer way to America, huh? The land of the free? Well, there you go!" The sailor gave him a vicious kick in the rear. Werner stumbled down the gangplank and fell flat on the pier.

So that's how he first reached America. On his hands and knees. Not a soft landing! No, indeed!

Chapter Nine

Sore from his tumble onto the pier, Werner picked himself up and glanced around. The passengers had all left, but there were plenty of dockworkers. Hard at work, they jabbered to one another in English. He listened close. How strange it sounded. Now he wished he'd learned a little from Anika. Then he could speak to people and ask questions.

Werner sank down on a barrel to wait. An hour dragged by, then another. Nothing to do and no one to talk to even if he knew how. He chewed on his fingernails. How long should he stay here? The rest of the day? All night?

Small white clouds scuttled across a clear blue sky. Gusts of cold damp air blew across the choppy water and onto the pier. Werner wrapped his blue jacket tightly around himself, murmuring, *Mutti, please keep me warm, keep me safe.*

He remembered, years ago, being with his mother in a busy train station. Somehow their hands were pulled apart and he could no longer see her. Small and terrified, he had stared through a forest of legs, boots, coats, umbrellas, and suitcases. Nobody looked friendly or familiar. He began screaming, *"Mutti, Mutti"*…until he heard his mother's gentle voice, *"Werner, mein Liebling, here I am."* He ran into her open arms….

"Werner Berlinger?" A short man in a brown suit stood in front of him, observing him with small suspicious eyes. The man's dark hair stuck up in tufts all over his head.

"*Ja, ja, ich heisse Werner!*" The boy jumped up and stammered. Yes, my name is Werner!

The short man didn't smile. "Show me your papers," he demanded in German.

Werner quickly pulled his documents from his pockets and handed them over.

The man studied the passport photograph, then squinted at the boy. "I guess you're him," he muttered gruffly and stuck out his hand. "I'm Conrad. Come with me."

With no further instruction, the short man took off walking at a fast pace. Werner followed as best he could. It wasn't easy. On all sides, Werner was surrounded by fast-talking, fast-walking people. The crowds were so thick you could barely stick a butter knife between one person and another. He began jogging to keep up, for if he slowed for an instant, somebody pushed from behind or knocked past him.

The city's noises pounded in his ears: horns blasting, trucks and taxis rumbling past. Most of all, the air was filled with people yelling to one another. Greetings, curses, people bargaining for this or that. From the varied sounds, he knew they were speaking different languages. He gazed around at the faces. Who could they be? Russian? Chinese? Spanish? Italian? How could so many different people live together in one place? In Germany, anyone foreign was viewed with suspicion and often shunned or avoided. Germans prized what was purely German. Yet here, no one seemed to care how you looked or what you sounded like. It seemed as if everyone was too busy to care!

The street was as crowded as the sidewalk – cars, trucks, taxis, trams. Even horse-drawn wagons! Each pressed forward a few inches at a time. People spilled from the sidewalks into the streets, squeezing between vehicles, still talking or shouting. No one had time to wait, even to eat. A huge woman wearing very high heels snacked on a sandwich as she teetered past. An old man shuffled along, chomping on peanuts from a sack and spitting out the shells. Young people swigged bottles of soda pop, while children tore off candy wrappers and stuffed the candy in their mouths.

After a few minutes, Werner passed two soldiers standing on the corner. They were eating frankfurters slathered with relish and mustard. Just seeing soldiers in uniform made the boy's stomach quake. But when he glanced back, one of the soldiers smiled and winked at him. Werner's mouth dropped open. A friendly soldier? Who would imagine such a thing!

He scrambled along behind the man in the brown suit. Buildings rose high on both sides – five, ten, fifteen, forty, seventy stories. On some streets, the sky was a mere stripe of blue between the buildings. There was so much to see, smell, hear, and touch. And everything seemed to shout: *You're in New York. You're in New York. You're in New York now!*

He wished he could stop and stare, to ask questions and explore. But Conrad walked quickly, never glancing back. At one point, he disappeared entirely. Werner craned his head, trying to catch a glimpse of Conrad. Then Werner paused, which way should he go now? Should he wait for Conrad to return?

A big, burly man bumped into him from behind. "Whatcha think you're doing, kid?" he snarled. Though Werner didn't understand the words, he could guess what they meant.

No. He couldn't wait. He had to keep going, even if he didn't know where. Finally, across the street and down the block, Werner glimpsed the brown tufts of hair on a head in the crowd. Rushing into the street to catch up, he headed straight into a line of vehicles. A bright yellow cab screeched to a stop. The driver leaned hard on the horn and yelled loudly. Werner glanced back but didn't dare slow down.

The short man in the brown suit didn't seem to notice. He kept walking, and Werner finally caught up. Ten minutes later, Conrad turned and entered a little store. The shelves were jammed with cans of food. Baskets of fruit, potatoes, and vegetables lined one wall. On the other were bins of bread – round bread, flat bread, rolls, bagels, twists, black bread, brown bread, rye bread – German bread. Werner gazed at the loaves with wonder. He wanted to pick one up, to feel its weight, and inhale its rich odor. The smell brought a pang of hunger to his gut and a sharp pain to his heart. How often he'd gone to the market and fetched bread like that. How often Father, Bettina, and he had made a meal of bread and cheese or bread and herring. Oh, how he wished they were with him now.

"That's him, Mr. Mozer. The young guy, the *schlimiel*, that Esther sent for," said Conrad, jerking his thumb toward Werner. "He don't look like much, but there he is." He spoke in Yiddish.

Mr. Mozer had white hair and thick glasses. He leaned over and peered at the boy. "*Sholem aleichem*. Welcome, young man, you've come a long way."

Werner gazed at him. Those were the first kind words he'd heard since arriving in America.

Chapter Ten

M r. Mozer's grocery store felt warm and friendly, but Werner didn't have long to enjoy the feeling. Conrad signaled for him to follow, and the two went out of the store to a hallway next door. They climbed two, three, four floors. The stairwell was dark and smelled of fried onions and sauerkraut. The banister beneath Werner's hand felt gritty with dirt and grease.

Finally, Conrad stopped in front of a battered blue door and raised his hand to knock. Then he paused, turning to Werner, and his voice was harsh. "Look, you *greenhorn*, maybe you think you've come to America to have a good time. Maybe you wanna make friends, play ball, and have fun. That's all American kids wanna do – play and have fun! But I want you to know right now." He stuck his face close to Werner's. "You came to help *her*, you see? She needs your help and you're gonna do whatever she needs! Understand?"

When Werner nodded, Conrad turned and knocked hard on the door. His voice changed from the harsh, commanding voice he'd used on Werner. It was now high and chirpy, filled with care and love. "Esther, Esther, sweetie, you in there?" he cooed.

A soft voice responded, *"Kommen Sie hinein!"* Please come in.

The two entered a small but neat apartment. Werner could still hear the noise of traffic outside the window, but inside a sense of calm and stillness reigned. A wonderful aroma filled the air. It took Werner only a few seconds to guess what it was – *Nudel kugel* – noodles baked in sweet cottage cheese with plump raisins. How Werner loved that smell. His mother had baked the dish often as a special treat. Bettina adored it. He imagined her here at this moment sniffing the air with delight.

A woman in a wheelchair sat near the window. Her skin was pale, as though it hadn't seen the sun in a long time. The smile lighting up her gentle face, however, was like a lullaby.

"You wanted him, here he is, Esther," the short man said gruffly, and pushed the boy toward her.

"How very glad I am," said the woman. "Please come here, dear Werner."

He walked toward her. Esther's long hair, pulled back in a bun, was fair but streaked with grey. Her eyes were light, too, a soft blue. She gently took his hand. "You look so much like your mother," Esther said. "It takes me back many years."

Werner tried to remember what Father had said. How did this strange woman in America know his mother? Seeing the boy's puzzled look, Esther spoke again, "Your mother, Hannah, was my first cousin, so I knew her well. We spent many happy holidays together until my family moved here. That was a long time ago, though, so perhaps you never heard of me."

Werner shook his head. He could remember so little of what his mother had said. Often she had talked of her childhood, her family and friends. But he hadn't bothered to listen, not knowing that she wouldn't always be there to tell about her life. He couldn't recall hearing about any cousins in the United States.

"I was very sad when I heard of her illness and death."

Werner's gaze dropped. He stared at Esther's thin, pale hands lying quietly in her lap.

"I would have come to see your family then, except for this." She tapped the arm of the wheelchair.

At the mention of the wheelchair, Conrad shifted restlessly. "I gotta be going, Esther. You know it ain't my usual day." He frowned. "Hope this young guy doesn't cause you any trouble. No trouble at all." He glared at Werner for a second and then looked back at Esther. "Here's his documents. I'll be back next week, as usual."

She nodded and smiled graciously at him. He received her smile like a dog lifting its head for a bone. "Thanks, Conrad," she murmured. "You are always so good to me."

Once he was gone, Esther gazed thoughtfully at Werner, then gestured around the small, plain room. "This probably wasn't what you were expecting," she said. "Most people think all Americans are rich. I wish it were so."

Again, Werner's eyes dropped, and he stared at his oversized boots. What had he been expecting? He wasn't sure. He didn't expect a palace, of course, but perhaps he had hoped for more than this. The apartment appeared to be one room for cooking and living plus a bathroom. Esther's bed was in the corner, piled with pillows. Newspapers were scattered on the floor around the bed. There was a tall bookshelf with books on every shelf, a small kitchen table, and a few chairs. A narrow cot was pushed against the wall near the icebox. He guessed that he'd sleep there.

The room was far bigger than the ship's cabin and far nicer than the orphanage. But it wasn't nearly as large and pleasant as his family's home. Was this what Father had dreamed about when he bought Werner a ticket to America? And what would Werner write about the place? Could he honestly say there was enough room here for Bettina and Father? Could they all squeeze together in this little space?

Of course they could! And they would! Father and Bettina had to follow him here. They had to know what it felt like to be in a free country. He'd only just landed, but Werner already knew. Crossing the city, he had seen hundreds of people. Some had been Jewish, no doubt. Yet not one person had a yellow star sewn onto their jackets. Not one walked with his shoulders hunched up, guarding himself from a cruel look or sharp blow.

And he recalled that soldier, the one who had been eating a frankfurter, and who had smiled and winked at him. How amazing! To walk across a huge, bustling city with no fear in your gut. That was worth the most difficult trip. That's why Father and Bettina must come too. He would write as soon as possible. He would make sure they came.

Without saying a word, Werner raised his eyes to meet Esther's. Seeming to understand, she smiled, "It's good you've come. Very good."

He smiled back. There was only one thing lacking at that moment. His stomach yearned for a big dish of Nudel kugel. The sooner the better!

Chapter Eleven

Werner awoke with a start. From habit, his hand felt the sheets beneath. Just in case. The sheets were *dry*, thank goodness. His muscles relaxed a bit, but only a little. Even though everything seemed fine, how could he be sure? He wasn't used to smiles and sunshine. He expected a dark cloud to appear in the midst of a cloudless day.

Pale winter light shone softly through the window. The radiators panted, sending warm air into the room.

Turning his head on the pillow, Werner gazed across the room. Esther was still sleeping. Barely two weeks had passed before the word "*Mutti*" slipped out of his mouth while speaking to Esther. He was surprised to hear himself say it. Then he realized that a mother is not always someone who's kin to you – it can be the way a woman makes you feel when you're with her. Esther gave him that feeling.

16 October, 1939

Dear Father,

I am sure you will like Esther. She is a fine person and as kind to me as a mother. . . .

Werner paused and laid down the pen for a moment. How could he explain to his father about Esther? It was true that she was like a mother to him, but unlike an ordinary mother who cares for her child, Werner took care of her.

Esther had explained to him that ten years ago she caught

a disease called polio. The disease had robbed her muscles of strength. Now she had her "good days" and her "bad days." On her good days, she climbed out of bed, grabbed her crutches and limped around the apartment.

Werner picked up the pen.

Esther loves to feed me. She is so happy when I gobble up all the good food she has prepared. "You gotta fatten up those skinny bones," she says. She makes big pots of chicken soup on top of the stove. She bakes delicious desserts like Nudel-kugel or Brotort.

She has a canary named Mozart. He's a mere flutter of yellow feathers but Esther adores him. "Mozart is my hero," she says. "For my little bird, every day is wonderful. Don't you wish you felt that way?"

Again, he paused. He didn't want to tell Father about the bad days, when Esther was too weak to rise from bed. Then she called to Werner. "Please take the cloth off the canary's cage. It's morning and he wants to sing."

Even sweet cherries have pits, he figured, and no cherries were sweeter than Esther. Her heart was far too big for her weak chest. If any person anywhere had a problem, she yearned to help. On every floor of the building, Esther was looking out for someone – she knit socks for any new baby and crocheted shawls for all the old ladies.

Each morning Werner fixed her a cup of weak, sugary tea. He toasted a slice of bread and put it on a plate with a spoonful of strawberry jam. Often he helped her climb into her wheel-chair. Then he parked the wheelchair under Mozart's cage next to the window. She sat there all day, her hands busy mending or knitting while she hummed along with the little bird.

Late in the morning she'd smile. "I bet Mr. Mozer is done with the news."

Werner knew what that meant. At dawn, bundles of newspapers were dropped in front of the grocery store. Mr. Mozer unpacked them for customers, always reading four or five himself. Every day Werner sped down four flights of steps to fetch the papers Mr. Mozer had finished. "Here you go, Werner," said Mr. Mozer, handing him a stack. "Come back in an hour and I'll give you another."

Werner scanned the newspaper for words he could understand. Lots of people in the neighborhood still spoke the languages that they'd used in Europe before coming to the U.S. That's why you heard German, Yiddish, Russian, Italian, and Polish on the street. But Werner wanted to be American as soon as possible and that meant learning how Americans talked. He was hungry for every word!

For Esther, the newspapers were a gate to a world she couldn't visit on foot. She read for hours, studying every scrap of news and even the advertisements. "Why, looka here, Werner. You see this? A dozen eggs cost a dime! That's a scandal! I don't remember paying more than a nickel!"

Werner picked up his pen to write more....

Sometimes Esther tells me stories from the past.

"Did I tell you, Werner, that when we lived in the village of Buxtehude, my grandmother had forty chickens? Oh my Lord, those chickens ran her life. Black ones, white ones, red ones, even gold chickens. Grandmother called each by name. 'Greta, have you laid an egg today, you silly 'ole hen? You been lazy for three days. Lay

me an egg this minute!' And she was so strict,
the chickens usually obeyed." After telling me
this story, Esther laughs and laughs.

The news in the newspapers, however, was not a laughing
matter. Every day Esther combed the newspaper to find out
what was happening in Europe. Especially what was happening
to Jews. The words told a terrible story. Nazi soldiers were ad-
vancing from country to country, and wherever they went, Jews
were jailed, beaten, forced into work camps or killed outright.
Esther would slump over in her seat with the newspaper sliding
from her lap. Then she'd sit silent or weep for an hour or more.

Werner picked up the pen to finish his letter. No, he
couldn't tell Father everything. He might worry. He might even
hesitate to come! No, it was much better for Father to come
and find out for himself.

I believe you will like Cousin Esther very
much. And she's eager to meet you and Bettina.
She says often how much she'd love to have a
little girl here.
So PLEASE find a way to come. As soon as
you can!!

Kisses and hugs to Bettina.
Your son, Werner

As he stuck a U.S. stamp on the corner of the letter, he
dreamed of their arrival. How great it would be to show them
around New York City. How happy they all would be in their
safe new home!

Yet Werner soon learned – with a black eye and bloody
nose – that nothing is quite so perfect. Even in New York!

Chapter Twelve

Esther's apartment was located on Second Avenue, between 10th Street and 11th Street. Mr. Mozer liked to say that the neighborhood was mixed. That meant there were Poles, Russians, Czechs, Hungarians, Serbians, Albanians, Turks, and Armenians, plus a smattering of Irish and Italians. People weren't too poor or too rich. Almost everyone worked; they made stuff, fixed stuff or sold stuff. There were butchers, bakers, shoemakers, tailors, carpenters, printers, and plumbers. People worked from early until late. Even after dark, you could hear the racket from woodshops, the hum of sewing machines, and the cries of young boys hawking the evening news.

At first, Werner didn't explore the neighborhood much. He wasn't used to freedom. Not after a year in an orphanage. Before that, when he had lived at home with Father and Bettina, it was too dangerous to spend time outside. Trouble could show up anywhere at any time. That's why they all lived behind closed doors.

So for the first few weeks in the U.S., Werner didn't venture far from Esther's apartment.

One day, however, Esther sent him down to Mr. Mozer's grocery store. She wrote a list on a worn paper bag: 1 can of tomato soup, 1 box of saltine crackers, 1 can of sardines, and a chunk of yellow cheese. She dropped a few coins in the bottom. "Here, Werner, get what you can," she said. "Put the stuff in this old sack. No need to waste a new one."

He took the bag with the list, put on his mother's pale blue wool jacket and his father's big hiking boots, and went downstairs. Although the store was directly below, he had to step out on the street to enter.

Across the street were three boys about his age, just hanging out. He had seen them a few times before. He figured they were the types who were nice and polite as long as they were standing next to their mother. Without her, they weren't going to be so nice.

On this day, they stared rudely at Werner and muttered to one another. He paused for a second and stared back. That was a mistake. The three marched over. A tall boy with a pale, pimply face stuck his nose close to Werner. "Look at those big stupid boots," he sneered. "Whatcha gonna do with them? Clean out the barn?"

The other boy was small and dark. "I bet he never cleaned out any barn in his whole life. He's a sissy."

"Yeah," said the pimply one. "Look at his jacket! That's a girlie jacket, don't you think?"

The third boy was chunky, blonde, and not so quick. "I think it would look really good on my sister. Whatcha think, guys?" He turned to Werner. "Why don't you give it to me, *putz?*"

Even though the three spoke English, Werner knew what they wanted. He'd experienced similar assaults by boys in the Hitler Youth. He clutched the coat tightly. *"Nein, nein!"* he shouted at them. There was no way he was going to give up his mother's precious jacket. He made a dash for the store. It was only a few feet away, but at that very moment, a large woman with a heavy bag of groceries blocked the door. Seeing the squabble, she hurried away. But by then, the boys had trapped Werner outside the store. They were still hooting and pulling at the blue jacket. When Werner tried to push past them, a fight began. Everyone was hitting and kicking and punching at once. Outnumbered three to one, Werner was soon flat on the sidewalk. One of the boys held him down while the other pulled off his jacket. The paper bag was ripped open. Quarters rolled down the sidewalk.

There was no telling how bad a beating Werner was going to get, but at that moment another boy appeared. He was sturdy, with thick curly black hair and a wide flat nose. "Whatcha doing?" he demanded of the boys who were clobbering Werner. The three immediately stopped punching him.

"Nuttin', Sam. We weren't doing nuttin'," said the pimply one.

The little dark kid swept up some quarters from the sidewalk and offered them to the new boy. "Want some cash, Sam? Easy money. Help yourself."

Sam waved the boy aside. "Get lost, you creeps. I don't want any of your stupid money."

The three didn't delay. They grabbed the money and dashed down the street. They waved the coat between them like a banner. Meanwhile, Sam reached down and helped Werner up, bruised and miserable.

"What a bunch of dummies," Sam said, watching the boys run down the street. He turned back to Werner. "You okay?"

Werner nodded.

"You gotta stand up for yourself in this neighborhood, or else they think you're a sissy."

Understanding what Sam said, Werner could only reply in German. "*Ich bin kein Feigling.*"

"What's that mean?" Sam asked.

Mr. Mozer was now standing in the door, "He says he's not a coward."

"Yeah, well, tell him that he better learn how to use his fists," said Sam, showing off his own two. Glancing once again at Werner's injured face, he shook his head, then cockily strolled away. Like he had a high opinion of himself and knew other kids in the neighborhood did, too.

Mr. Mozer helped Werner inside. "What kind of a welcome is this? You deserve better." He dabbed at the blood on the boy's lower lip, now swollen and purple. "You came to the store to get something. Tell me, whatcha need?"

Werner handed over a scrap of brown paper, all that remained of the list. Mr. Mozer got the bread, sardines, cheese,
and a can of soup. In fact, he put an extra can of soup into a
brand-new paper bag. Then the two walked to the apartment
hallway. Werner's nose was leaking drops of blood. One eye was
puffy and nearly shut. He hunched over – how could he have
lost his mother's coat?

Seeing him upstairs, Esther gasped. "Werner, my poor darling, what happened?"

She hobbled to the icebox and wrapped a dishtowel around
a chunk of ice, pressing it to his eye. He sank down on his bed
and pulled off his father's boots. Then he shoved the heavy
boots far under the bed. He wasn't going to wear them again.
Not here on this street. The boots smelled like Germany, a
place that already seemed a lifetime away. As soon as possible
Werner would find a way to get a pair of flimsy black shoes like
the other boys wore. American shoes.

The rest of the day Esther fussed over him, fixing tomato
soup and crackers. Werner kept thinking of the three boys on
the street. He was no coward – he knew how to use his fists.
He had used them plenty back in Germany. But he wasn't expecting the same treatment here. Especially when the bullies
weren't Nazi youth who had been taught to hate Jews. They
were Jewish boys, just like him.

"I'm no sissy," he thought to himself. Still, he didn't want
to go looking for fights either. Not when the odds were three
against one. So he stayed put in the tiny apartment most of the
time. Some days were okay, but often he felt like a prisoner. A
prisoner living only a few miles from the Statue of Liberty, how
crazy was that?

The bullies on the street were one problem, but there was
another – much worse. Conrad Blusteiner. He came to visit
Esther every Sunday, arriving almost exactly at 3 p.m., rarely
more than a few minutes late. As soon as Werner opened the
door, his face screwed up in a tight frown. "Why don't you find

something to do, kid," he'd say and hand the boy a few cents.

Werner would go downstairs and buy a penny's worth of candy from Mr. Mozer. The store closed early on Sundays, but the grocer would be there anyway. He was a widower whose grown daughters lived far across the city. The store was the place he most liked to be.

"Whatcha want to do?" he'd ask Werner. "Listen to the radio or play pinochle?"

Usually they did both until they saw Conrad leave. Always in the same brown suit, with his head hunched low between his shoulders. He walked fast on his short legs, like he could leave his troubles behind if he moved quickly enough.

Werner was curious. Why was Conrad so devoted to Esther? Why was he so angry at Werner? He asked Mr. Mozer, but the grocer just shrugged. "You'll learn some day."

One afternoon, however, when Conrad was rushing past, he glanced up and saw Werner. He stopped short. "Hey, you bum," he said, "you know you're eating up the little money Esther has. The little she's got saved in the bank. I try to give her a bit extra to make up for what you eat, but it's not always enough, is it, Mr. Mozer?"

"It is nearly enough, Conrad," Mr. Mozer said gently.

"You think so?" Conrad sneered. "I don't. She was better off before that guy showed up to sponge off her."

He started to stalk off, then turned back to Werner. "I should send you back where you came from, that's what I oughta do."

"God forbid, Conrad, you should say such a horrible thing!" Mr. Mozer spoke sternly. "Shame on you."

That made Conrad button up his mouth, but the look he gave Werner as he left made the boy think he might do it. *He might send him back.*

Werner shuddered. Everyone in the neighborhood had heard about the SS *St. Louis*. Filled with Jews and other refugees from Europe, the ship had come to the port of New

York six months ago. But not one person had been allowed
to disembark. The unfortunate ship had traveled from port to
port seeking a place to unload its passengers. Yet every place
had turned it away. Not one city had allowed the hundreds of
people on board to walk down the gangplank to freedom and
safety. Instead, with nowhere else to go, the ship had turned
around and carried its poor passengers back to Europe. Back to
fear and danger and death.

Could such a terrible thing happen to him? Did Conrad
hate him that much?

Seeing Werner's misery, Mr. Mozer finally explained, "From
what I understand, Conrad married the wrong gal. He wanted
to marry Esther, but that didn't work out. Now he's stuck,
stuck with a wife he don't want to be with."

Werner thought for a moment. "But I still don't understand. Why does he hate me?"

Mr. Mozer shrugged. "He wishes he could be doing what
you're doing, living up there and helping Esther," he said.
"Conrad's jealous. Jealousy makes a person do mean things."

Mean things? Like sending him back to Germany? Werner
wondered if such a horrible thing was possible? When he went
upstairs, he tried to keep his stomach from growling. What
Conrad said was true – he did eat a lot. He was always hungry,
though he stayed thin as a broom pole, no matter how much
he stuffed himself. I will eat less, he swore to himself. *I won't
give Conrad any reason to send me back. None at all.*

Esther was propped up on pillows in bed. She was wearing
a thin silk kimono and sipping a little glass of *kirsch*, the sweet
cherry brandy Conrad brought her as a gift. Her eyes looked
puffy and pink. Werner guessed that she'd been crying. She
patted the mattress next to her and he sat down. "You deserve
so much more, Werner. You deserve a mother that can take you
places, do things for you." Esther smiled sadly. "A real *Mutti*."

Werner shook his head. "No, Esther, I like it here. I like being here with you."

Esther patted his hand, "Don't worry about Conrad. He doesn't understand. He doesn't know how good you are to me."

Werner looked around the little apartment. What more could he do to help? Already he cleared out Mozart's cage every day, letting the little flutter of bright yellow fly freely as he worked. He cleaned the kitchen until it was so tidy, a mouse couldn't find a crumb. He scrubbed and scrubbed the bathtub until it shined, although the bottom still had big bluish green stains. Every night, the tub was filled with hot water so Esther could soak her aching muscles.

What else could he do? Werner jumped up and rolled up some old newspapers to shove under the door. Keeping out drafts was an important job. The apartment had to stay warm and dry. Esther was terrified of catching even a little cold. "The polio hurt my chest bad," Esther said. "For months I lay in a machine called an iron lung to help me breathe. It was the only way I could sleep. Otherwise I'd stop breathing."

Werner stared at her in horror. Stop breathing? That meant she'd die. That would be horrible. Too awful to imagine. But what if it did happen? With Esther gone, Conrad would send him back to Germany for sure. There'd be nobody here to help Father and Bettina!

Werner didn't dare speak to Esther about his worries. She had enough of her own. But he wished he had someone to talk to. He thought of Anika. Where was his friend now? She might cheer him up with her bright laughter and charm. Of course, he knew there was little chance of ever seeing her again, not in this gigantic city filled with millions of people. Then he thought of his buddies at the orphanage – Lutz, Mandel, Sammel, and Victor. How terrific it would be to glimpse even one of their friendly faces! That's all he needed – one chum, just one buddy.

Chapter Thirteen

When Werner did make a friend, it was a big surprise. The day was November 29, unbelievably cold, colder than he could remember, even during Germany's cruel winters. And wet, too. Wind blew frozen rain across the buildings and stores. People on the sidewalk were bundled in heavy coats, thick scarves, gloves, hats, and boots. They rushed from one doorway of a shop to another, hoping to grab a little shelter or a blast of warm air when a door opened.

Werner was heading down the block to the newsstand to see which comic books had arrived. The cold didn't bother him much because now he had a warm coat. Esther had gotten it from Mr. Todeskie who lived two floors down. Mr. Todeskie got it cheap from his son who worked in the Garment District across town where thousands of coats were made. One sleeve was slightly shorter than the other, which is why it was such a bargain. But, for Werner, the coat seemed perfect – snug and stylish – a true American coat.

He walked down the street boldly. In such freezing weather, the neighborhood bullies didn't hang out on the corner. So, he wasn't worried that anyone would jump out and steal the nickels in his pocket.

At the newsstand, the vendor knew just what he wanted. "Look at these, boy." He eagerly pointed to a stack. "Just arrived, a brand new series of comics, fresh from the printer."

Werner picked up one. The cover showed an exciting sea battle with a Nazi flag flying over a ship. *MARVEL* was the name on top in big red letters. He handed over two nickels, then stuck the comic book under his arm and started back, eager to begin reading. He ducked his head against the driving sleet, thinking how nice it would be to curl up on top of his bed in the warm apartment. Mozart would be chirping away while thick potato and cabbage soup bubbled on the stove.

He'd only traveled a block when he saw the boy who had come to his aid several weeks before. He remembered the boy's name, "Sam." The bullies had clearly respected Sam who, at the time, had seemed cocky and confident. Today, however, he didn't look so tough, quite the opposite. He was sitting on the edge of the street curb, shivering so hard his cap was sliding off his black curls. His chin was pressed to his chest, his arms wrapped tight around each other for warmth. And no wonder, he wasn't wearing a coat or jacket of any sort. His nose was scarlet red and his cheeks were soaked, not from rain, but from tears! His chin trembled and he kept wiping the snot dripping from his nose.

Werner couldn't believe it. The proud, cocky kid Sam was crying! Bawling!

Embarrassed for him, Werner quickly looked away. But not fast enough. Sam glanced up. Immediately, the boy's lower lip bulged and his body stiffened. "Whatcha looking at me for, ya dope?"

Werner knew he could just walk away. In fact, that was the safest thing to do, for sure. Yet Sam looked too unhappy, too miserable. And Werner knew those feelings well. So he stayed, planted to the sidewalk, wishing he could speak enough English to ask what was wrong. Icy rain pelted the two boys; Werner pushed his hands further into his pockets for warmth. At the bottom of one, he felt the hard edge of the nickel left after buying his comic.

"You wanna eat sumptin'?" he muttered to Sam.

The first words Werner had learned involved food and eating. That's about all he could say. Then he pointed to Liesel's Bakery on the corner. The smell of freshly baked bread, cinnamon rolls, and donuts wafted down the street from the bakery.

Sam glanced at the bakery, then scowled, like he might say no. His pride was clearly wrestling with his stomach. And Werner knew that hunger wins out every time.

"Sure, okay." Sam stood up, still shivering. "Better than sitting here doing nuttin'."

The two walked to the Swiss bakery and sat at the counter. With his nickel, Werner bought two donuts, covered with powdery white sugar, and a cup of black coffee. He poured lots of cream into the cup and heaped in spoonfuls of sugar before pushing it toward Sam. Though the cup was still steaming hot, Sam gulped down nearly half. He was that cold.

After a moment, however, he unfroze enough to talk. Werner listened closely, understanding only half the words but most of what Sam meant. "Every payday my dad gets loaded on whiskey, you see," he explained. "Then he starts yelling at me or my mom. Mostly it's me he beats up. A few times, he's thrown me down the stairs. Nowadays, I head out the door as soon as I smell whisky on his breath."

"Here? The street?" Werner pointed out the door.

"Sure, I hang out with the bums for a few days," said Sam. "It's not so bad as you think. I wouldna go back at all 'cept for Mom. She'd have it miserable if I left for good. I'm the oldest, you see. And she's got five younger."

Most times, he claimed, he did okay. But today the weather was so damn lousy, filthy, cold and wet. Plus he'd run out the door with nothing but the shirt on his back.

"You think I'd go back and ask Dad for a jacket?" Sam stuck out his bottom lip. "Then you don't know me, Sam Ublentz." He glanced at Werner. "I'm no *crybaby* neither. I just hit a real bad moment back there." He jerked his thumb toward the curb outside where he'd been sitting.

Werner nodded. Even when tears don't show, he knew, they grow in your heart. It's often better to let them flow freely. A little smile turned up the corners of his mouth. How good it felt, for once, to be helping somebody else.

When the boys had finished every drop of coffee and every donut crumb, they went to Esther's apartment. As soon as Werner introduced her to Sam, she was her kindhearted self.

"Run the hot water in the tub," she commanded Werner, and then turned to Sam. "You poor *boychik*, take a long soak."

She rummaged around until she found dry clothes and some thick socks she'd knitted. In less than an hour, Sam was fast asleep on Werner's cot, snoring loudly. When he woke up, they all ate potato cabbage soup. Sam downed three bowlfuls, one after the other.

Meeting up with Sam marked a big change for Werner. Everyone in the neighborhood, young and old, girls and boys, respected and liked Sam. It was hard not to. He grinned easily, showing off a gap in his mouth where his dad had knocked out a front tooth. His black hair was so thick it looked as if the curls were wrestling for a spot on his head. His nose was big and flat, though he bragged that it was not yet broken. Sam wasn't the smartest kid on the block, but he was known to be honest, affectionate, and reliable.

With Sam as his pal, the bullies on the street didn't dare bother Werner. And with a pal to talk to, his English improved rapidly. Words came in bits, then chunks. Soon he was speaking whole sentences. He spoke New York style, in a rush, and not always proper English. But what did that matter? What counted was that now he could get a job and a real foothold in America....

28 October, 1939

Dear Father,

I have good news. Sam Ublentz is my friend. His family came from Czechoslovakia but Sam was born right here so he's a 100% American.

Soon I will be too. He's helping me learn English. Now I know a hundred words, at least. Soon I can get a job as a newsboy or shoeshine or store clerk that gets me real money. You should see the pocketfuls of change a newsboy takes home every day. There will be plenty for all of us — enough money, enough food, and a warm place to live. Buy your ticket today.

Esther sends her best. We both wish for the day when you both arrive.

Hugs and kisses to the sweetest sister in the world.
Your son, Werner

He wrote letters to his family every week, sometimes two or three times, but not one letter had arrived from them. Day after day, he rushed to see the mail. Again and again, he was disappointed.

"Don't worry, *bubele*," Esther said. "The war has slowed down the mail from Germany. You gotta keep writing. That's what gives your family hope."

But Werner knew she was worried, too.

Chapter Fourteen

One night Werner and Esther heard a knock on the door. "Who can that be?" she asked.

When Werner opened the door, a stocky man with grey whiskers and a reddish nose stood outside. Mr. Boronski, the neighborhood butcher, took off his cap. "Is…is Esther Bochmann here?" He stammered.

Esther looked up from darning a sock. "You know I am, Sol. Where else would I be?"

He grunted and shuffled his feet. "Can I come in?"

Esther smiled, "We only know each other for the past 20 years. Whatcha need?"

He came in and took a seat at the kitchen table, still holding his cap.

"Some of us noticed how you got this young fella out of Germany." He nodded toward Werner. "Some of us got kinfolk we'd like to get out, too."

Esther's smile faded. "I know you do. Most every family on the block has got somebody they want to get out. Sisters or brothers. Uncles, aunts, grandparents, cousins. Entire families."

Mr. Boronski nodded gravely and held up a thick pile of papers. "Did you hafta fill out all these?" he asked.

Esther counted eighteen pages of U.S. government forms. "My God, there's twice as many as I filled out six months ago. You sure you need 'em all?"

The butcher nodded again. "I been trying to get my niece out of Frankfurt for…for over a year." He pulled out a large handkerchief and blew his nose, then wiped tears from his eyes. "Her parents already are gone, God knows where, maybe killed. Me and my wife want to help out Sofia if we can." He shook his head. "She's only fourteen."

Esther was silent a moment. "Honest, Sol, I don't know what I can do. No miracles, for sure."

At the word "miracles," Mr. Boronski raised his hands high in the air. "Whatever you can do is what we want." He turned to Werner. "She got you out, kid, didn't she? She's a real heroine, like Esther in the story of Purim."

Esther scoffed at the idea that she could rescue Jews from Hitler the way the biblical Esther had rescued her people from the cruel tyrant Haman. The evil king had planned to kill all the Hebrew people in his empire, but the brave woman had outwitted him.

"There's a chance for Sofia," said Esther, "because she's only fourteen." It was the same opportunity, she explained, that had enabled her to get Werner into the United States. Some children under the age of sixteen were being allowed in the country. The quota for adults didn't seem to apply to these young people.

"That must be how Anika and the other children on the ship came here," added Werner.

Mr. Boronski left that evening, feeling hopeful. Word quickly spread. The next evening came another knock on the door. This time it was Tamara Ezekiel, who was trying to get her twin brother out of Poland. "I been to United States Immigration and Naturalization Services so many times, they're sick to see my face," claimed Tamara. "Please, Esther, please help me! He's my only brother. And he'll think I don't care."

Another unhappy person to climb the stairs was David Sesselbaum. His sweetheart had gone to college in Heidelberg, and now she couldn't get back.

"This is ridiculous," said Esther. "Nancy is an American citizen, even if she was born in Germany. They have to let her back in."

David was close to tears. "We gotta get her out. We got to!

I gotta see my gal again."

"Gimme those forms," demanded Esther. "I'll do what I can."

Working together, David and Werner laid out the forms on the floor. End-to-end they stretched across the apartment – nine full feet. And the government wasn't asking for just one copy – they wanted six of each. Every page copied by hand! Esther worked that night and every night for one neighbor after another. She'd grow so tired that her fingers cramped, her chin dropped to her chest, and she'd doze in the wheelchair.

Finally, Werner said, "I don't understand why we're helping everyone on the block, but we haven't filled out any forms for Father and Bettina!"

Esther gazed at him without speaking for a few seconds. "A year ago, I wrote your Father and told him I could try to get all of you out," she said, "but a month later he wrote back to me." Her eyes were teary. "He said you had a better chance of coming alone. Once you were safe, he'd figure out how to come with your sister."

For a moment, Werner couldn't speak. His chest felt so tight, he could hardly breath. Had his father purposely given up his chance to come, just for him? "Well, I'm here now," he burst out. "There's no reason why we can't get them out, too."

"You're right," said Esther. "Let's start right now."

When they'd filled out the applications for Father and Bettina, Werner was eager to take them to the Immigration and Naturalization Office.

Esther instructed him, "Stand at the counter 'til the clerk pays attention. Tell him you won't go 'til he marks the forms with a date. Then they can't say later that they didn't get 'em. Like they do lots of times."

Sam helped Werner find the big office building. When the boys reached the room, they saw people crowded together, lining the benches around the room. Some sat on the floor or paced in the hallway outside. Everyone, guessed Werner, was trying as hard as they could to get U.S. visas for people they loved.

After waiting over five hours, a man behind the counter called to Werner. The clerk had thick grey hair and bushy eyebrows. He took the packet of information like it was dirty laundry and started to turn away.

"Stamp it!" Werner insisted. "Put today's date on it. I wanna see you do it." The clerk tried to shoo the boy away, but Sam snapped, "You heard my friend. Stamp it now!"

The clerk finally stamped the documents, muttering, "The quota for many immigrants has been cut in half!"

"What?" Werner exclaimed.

"The State Department doesn't want people coming here taking jobs away from good Americans." His bushy eyebrows went up an inch. "The new quota applies to Jews, gypsies, thieves and undesirables."

"Undesirables?" Werner repeated in a low angry voice. Esther had read aloud the newspaper article about Albert Einstein, a brilliant German scientist who had recently been welcomed to the United States. Since Einstein was Jewish, why wasn't he considered an "undesirable"?

Werner's feet dragged as he walked down the marble steps of the office building. Sam bought him a root beer soda to try to cheer him up, but even his favorite drink didn't lift his mood.

"How can this be?" Esther moaned when she heard. "The great United States of America once promised: *Give me your tired, your poor, your huddled masses yearning to breathe free.* She shook her head sadly. "Those are the words writ in big letters on the Statue of Liberty. But now our own country is closing its gates. And if we shut the door, so will every country in the world."

For once, Werner had no appetite at all. Still, he opened a can of tomato soup and poured the contents into a pot. He had squeaked into the U.S. through a crack. So had other Jewish children like Anika and the other youngsters on the ship. But what about everyone else? What about Father and Bettina and Anika's father? What would happen to them?

"I can't believe the president knows what's happening," Esther exclaimed. "If President Roosevelt had any idea, he'd do something."

Werner added milk and stirred the soup, watching the little bubbles rise to the top.

Franklin D. Roosevelt was now his president, too. Most people loved him, especially people in their neighborhood because he helped poor people. Maybe, Werner thought, the president doesn't know. He doesn't know there are thousands and thousands of people in Europe who urgently need his help.

"We can write him a letter."

"What?" Esther asked.

"We can write the president a letter. Then he'll know. Then he'll do something."

"That's a wonderful idea, Werner. But I can make it even better," Esther smiled broadly. "We'll write Mrs. Roosevelt. She reads her mail, I know, and she talks a lot to her husband."

The two worked on the letter together. Esther wrote it all down in good English.

When he went down to mail the letter, Esther smiled, "You're a real *mensch*, Werner. And already such a good American!"

For the first time that day, Werner felt happy.

Chapter Fifteen

Soon after that, Werner started school. Esther had always urged him to go, but he had delayed for two big reasons. Number one, he didn't want to look stupid. He had missed years of school in Germany after schools stopped permitting Jewish students to attend. At the orphanage, an instructor showed up only a few days a week. Werner had always been a good reader and wrote well enough. But in the subjects of math, history, and geography, he figured he was far behind.

Another reason was Conrad. The guy had made it clear that Werner's *only* excuse for being in the United States was caring for Esther. If he went to school, Conrad might decide he was useless. What might happen then? Werner didn't like to think about it.

Still, he didn't want to be a greenhorn his whole life. He had to learn how to speak right, to read English. And he badly wanted a job. Then he could buy groceries for Ester and not be so useless. But to get any job, he needed to know how to count money and read labels.

So one grey, blustery morning Werner headed for school. He knew just where to go – New York Public School 122. A few minutes later, he stood on the steps of a large square brick building. Inside, he could hear a jumble of children's voices and the clatter of little feet. An adult yelled, "No running in the hall!"

Taking a deep breath, Werner climbed the steps and pushed open the heavy door. The wide hallway was empty; the students were now back in their classrooms.

He had barely stepped onto the polished wooden floor,

however, when a plump man with a round face and thin dark mustache asked, "Who are you? And what are you doing here, young man?"

"I'm...I'm Werner Berlinger. And I...I wanna go to school," Werner mumbled.

The man gazed at him sharply, then stuck out a hand. "I'm Mr. Stromboski, the school principal. Have you ever been to school before?"

Werner shook his head. "Not in America."

Mr. Stromboski's little mustache twitched. "Then please come with me," he commanded, leading Werner into his office and handing him a piece of paper. "Now sit down and fill this out." It was a short test.

The principal watched as the boy struggled to read and answer the questions. Werner finally handed the quiz back to Mr. Stromboski. The paper was mostly smudges and blank spaces.

"Hmmm," said Mr. Stromboski, examining the test while stroking his thin mustache. "Please follow me."

He led Werner down the long wide hall. Finally, he stopped and opened the door to a classroom filled with tiny children, younger than his sister. Mr. Stromboski nudged Werner inside. "Here's where you belong for now, in the first grade."

Werner stared at the young children. His face and hands felt hot and sweaty. He turned and glared at Mr. Stromboski. "You can't stick me with these little kids."

"I'm sorry, young man," said the principal, looking genuinely sorry. "This is the class you belong in because of your skills. You will be moved to another class as soon as you are able to do the work."

Werner opened his mouth to protest, then shut it. He slunk into the room and sat down at a little desk. The tiny chair beneath him wobbled. His knees didn't fit beneath the desk. All the first graders stared at him and giggled to one another until the teacher warned them to stop.

So what, Werner thought, *I don't care*. I will sit at this little desk all day, every day, for weeks, or months, or years. If that's what it takes to become a real American, to get a foothold in this country and bring my family here!

Sam and the other kids his age hooted every time they passed by and saw him hunched over his little desk. The first graders, however, loved having such a big boy in the class. They became Werner's pals and willing slaves. "Go sharpen my pencil, Joey," he'd command, and the youngster would instantly obey. "Pass me an eraser, Nina," he'd demand, and a tiny girl would toss him one.

The best part of first grade, however, was his teacher, Mrs. Elinore McIntosh. She was solid and strong as a farmer's wife and plenty strict. "What is your name?" she asked that first day.

"W-Werner Berlinger," he said.

"Please repeat after me: 'My name is Werner,'" she commanded. From then on, he could never just say "yes" or "no." She insisted that he answer every question in a complete sentence. He worked hard to learn to speak, and read and write in English. After only six weeks, Mrs. McIntosh said, "You know everything I can teach you in first grade, Werner. It's time for you to try second grade."

Werner frowned. "But I like it here, Mrs. McIntosh. Please, let me stay."

She smiled. "You are a hardworking student. Come to my room at lunchtime every day for thirty minutes. We will continue your lessons." She looked at him sternly. "No goofing off, no excuses, Werner. You must come every day." And he did.

19 December, 1940

Dear Father,

I go to school five days a week and spend every lunchtime studying, too. There's so much to learn. Not just in class. Everything here is different. For example, twice a day, kids line up for their turn at the "water fountain" — such a neat invention. At lunch, we eat from trays in a cafeteria instead of going home for a meal. You see, like everyone in New York, we kids are too busy to go home in the middle of the day.

And imagine this — I sit next to <u>a girl</u> in class because girls and boys go to the same school. And when the teacher asks a question, girls raise their hands same as boys — and they know the right answer too. Just as often as boys.

Most important, I am learning English. Everywhere I go I read everything I can — the newspaper, street signs, the ingredients on soup cans.

Next week we stay home a whole week for Christmas. And I will so miss school and my new friends. Yesterday all the students sang Christmas carols, even the Jewish students. And no one seemed to mind or even notice.

Last night Esther and I lit candles for Chanukah. We prayed you will be here soon. There are many Jewish families on this street so you can see candles in window after window! It is beautiful and fills my heart with hope.

Many hugs and kisses for my dear sister.
Your son, Werner

One day, as usual, he carefully put his letter in the thin blue envelope for overseas mail. He took it to the postbox on the corner and dropped it in. Turning to leave, however, he saw someone staring at him. The man was tall, completely bald, and wore thick spectacles. He had a pipe clamped tightly between his teeth. "Do you know who I am?" The man spoke in German. Werner gritted his teeth. Nowadays he hated even the sound of German; it reminded him of so many bad times. In fact, he had already forgotten many German words in his rush to learn English. And he was glad, glad to forget.

Still, he couldn't pretend he didn't understand. He knew the man's name was Oscar Buddorf and that he owned a tobacco store on the corner. So he nodded.

"Well, I know who you are, too." Mr. Buddorf almost hissed the words. "You came here from Germany and you are a Jew."

Werner couldn't see the man's eyes through his thick glasses.

"I belong to a group called the *Amerika Deutscher Bund.* Do you know what that means?" asked Mr. Buddorf.

When Werner shook his head, the tall bald man explained, "We come from Germany and we are very proud of being German." His mouth slid into a crooked smile. "We are also proud of Adolph Hitler. He is the best thing that has happened to Germany in a long time. Germany is strong again and Germans are happy."

For a moment, Werner thought Mr. Buddorf was going to click his heels together, straighten his arm and say "*Heil Hitler.*" But he didn't. He just curled his lips into an ugly sneer. "That letter you just dropped in the box…you think it will reach your family?"

Werner couldn't speak for a moment. "Sure…sure it will," he stammered. "Why won't it?"

Oscar Buddorf didn't answer. Instead, he made a funny noise, as if he were laughing, though it sounded more like choking. Then he turned and strode back to his little shop on the corner.

Watching him go, Werner felt like a huge ugly spider was crawling up his back. How did Mr. Buddorf know his name? Did the Bund know the name of every German who came to the United States? And what did Mr. Buddorf know about his family? Did he know something that Werner didn't know?

Werner couldn't bear standing there another second. He turned and started running and didn't stop until he was back in Esther's apartment with the door firmly latched.

Chapter Sixteen

As soon as Werner could read, write, and count well enough, he got a job at Mr. Mozer's grocery store. Every afternoon he stacked cans on shelves, poured bags of onions and potatoes into bins, swept floors, wiped off counters, and helped customers carry heavy bags to the door.

"When you know your way around town better," said Mr. Mozer, "I'll lend you a bike so you can deliver the groceries to people's homes. People like that and you'll make extra on tips."

One of his chores at the end of every day was carrying the garbage bags to the alley behind the store. Sometimes he'd see a hobo out there, scrounging for food. That's how he met Alf.

Just as he was slamming the lid down on a garbage can, a giant of a man loomed up in the dark alley. Werner froze with fear. The man's skin was dark as coffee. His hair was black and hung down his back in a single long braid. He wore a dingy pair of overalls over a ragged flannel shirt. Underneath, Werner could see that his muscles were as big as Tarzan's – one of his favorite comic strips and movie heroes. But not one he expected to meet in a dark alley.

"You skeered of me, kid?" the big man mumbled.

Werner could barely nod.

"You should be," said the giant. "I'm half Eskimo, half Negro, half Navajo, and part skunk." The man laughed loudly, then stuck out his big paw. "People call me Alf. What do people call you?"

"W-Werner," the boy stammered. In Germany he had never even seen a black person, much less talked to one. The pictures he'd seen in books, however, portrayed African cannibals. They were savage beings who cooked up missionaries in big pots and then ate them. Since coming to New York, he'd seen many Negroes: carpenters, seamstresses, a truck driver, a teacher. But he'd always stayed a safe distance away.

Now his arm was shaking as he reached out and grasped a few of Alf's dingy fingers. "H-h-how do you do, sir?"

Alf laughed loudly, "Why, listen to you calling me 'sir'! You're some kinda polite kid."

From then on, Alf visited often to see what kind of food was in Mr. Mozer's garbage cans. He'd search for mushy fruit, out-of-date cans and stale bread. Sometimes Werner put stuff like this on the side, just in case Alf showed up.

Alf brought junk to Werner that he'd found on the streets and alleys. Good stuff like a baseball glove with the stitching missing or a wooden bat only slightly cracked. Best of all, he told the boy stories about growing up out West with wild horses, grizzly bears and rattlesnakes.

Werner couldn't hear enough about this wild, free boyhood, so different from his own. "How come you ended up here, Alf?" he often asked.

Looking around, the giant man seemed surprised. "I ain't sure how I got here."

Werner shook his head. How could anyone trade a home in the mountains and prairies for a stinky, dark New York alley?

One late afternoon, Sam was helping Werner take out the garbage when Alf arrived. The big man's eyes shone with excitement. "Hey, boys, looka here what I found!" He pulled out a dented wood crate.

"Yuck," Werner said, holding his nose. A sick aroma like overripe melons or bananas filled the air. But then he leaned in close to look. What was in there? He couldn't see a thing.

"It's alive," Alf exclaimed.

Werner stepped back. "Not a rat?"

The giant man looked disgusted. "For crying out loud, Werner, why would anybody put a filthy rat in a box?"

Sam guessed this time. "A cat, a kitten." There were always stray cats around, chasing rats in the alleys or snagging fish heads at the market.

"Much better than a pussycat!" said Alf, starting to grin.

"I give up," Werner exclaimed. "Let's see."

Alf reached into the box and lifted out a live creature. Something neither boy had ever seen before, except in books. He handed it to Werner.

"A turtle!" Sam exclaimed. "Where did you find a turtle?"

Alf shook his big head, his eyes filled with wonder. "Can you believe a little turtle like that could be living on the streets of New York?"

He gently touched the turtle's shell. "I used to find these critters all the time when I was a boy in Montana, but *here* in New York?"

The three gazed at the turtle in Werner's hands. Its head stuck out and so did its stubby little feet. They were speechless thinking of all the things that could destroy a turtle as it marched slowly across the city. Taxis, trucks, trolleys, wagons, police on horseback. How did the turtle get here? How come it was still alive?

Sam knocked on the shell of the turtle. "Pretty tough little guy." He looked at Alf. "You gonna keep him?" His eyes were dark with longing.

Alf considered a moment, then shrugged. "Nah, I don't need no turtle. I had plenty of turtles when I was your age. Other good stuff too – lizards, crows, possums. You take him."

11 March, 1940

Dear Father,
 You can't guess how lucky I am. I have my own pet. Our friend Alf gave me and Sam a box turtle named Julius Caesar. We named

him ourselves. Sam has been studying about the Roman general Julius Caesar. His teacher says that one of the most amazing things Caesar ever did was cross the Rubicon. It was incredibly brave, even for a tough Roman general. We're not sure what the Rubicon is, but we figure for a turtle to cross New York City is equally difficult or more so.

Of course, both of us wanted to keep Julius in our homes. But Sam was worried about his father. He said, "What if dad gets drunk one day and hurls Julius down the stairwell? Six floors onto a hard floor could crack his shell."

So we put the turtle's crate behind the heater in Esther's apartment. The space is tiny but warm. I can easily find enough onion peels, wilted lettuce and carrot scrapings to feed Julius. Esther doesn't mind my having a turtle, though she refers to him as the "reptile."

Every morning I thump on his shell and say, "Are you coming out today, Julius?" Sometimes he does, and then he dashes around the apartment faster than you can imagine. But on the days he doesn't want to come out, there's no way I can entice him. Not with juicy carrots or soda crackers or grapes.

Life in America, you see, is filled with surprising and happy events. I look forward to the day when you and Bettina meet Julius in person. Bettina may be scared at first but she will grow to love him like I do.

100 kisses to Bettina.
Your son, Werner

For a boy who'd never before had a pet, who had barely dreamed that he could *ever* have a pet, Julius was perfect. In fact, there wasn't much Werner wouldn't do for his little turtle.

Chapter Seventeen

First grade had been wonderful because of Mrs. McIntosh. Werner skipped from her class to third grade and two months later moved to fourth grade. None of the teachers were as great as Mrs. McIntosh but none were evil, either. Not until Werner reached fourth grade. Then every minute in class, he felt like dirt was being kicked in his face. Who kicked the dirt? The fourth grade teacher, Nathanial Pendergrast.

From the first minute Werner walked through the door, he knew he was in trouble.

Seeing him enter, five inches taller than any other fourth grader, Mr. Pedergrast's face twisted into a peculiar smile.

"New boy!" the teacher called loudly, rapping on his desk with a ruler and gesturing for him to come forward.

Unsure what was happening, Werner hesitated, pointing to himself. "Me, sir?"

Mr. Pendergrast nodded. "Yes, you, come to the front right now."

Werner walked up slowly, little hairs rising on the back of his neck. The other fourth graders stared but didn't dare giggle.

Once he stood in front of Mr. Pendergrast, the teacher gazed down at his class list. "I see your name here," he said very loudly and clearly. "It's Werner Berlinger." The teacher gave him a sharp look.

"Yes, s-sir," Werner stammered.

"*Werner*," Mr. Pendergrast repeated slowly. The way he said it, the word sounded odd. A few students at the back of the room tittered and nudged one another. "What do you think, class? Does Werner sound like an *American* name?" The teacher's mouth curled into a sneer beneath his bristly grey mustache.

Before Werner had a chance to reply, however, Mr. Pendergrast answered his own question. "I don't think so. I don't think Werner is an American name."

The boy frowned. "What is an American name, sir?" he asked politely.

"You ask me what is an American name?" Mr. Pendergrast's eyes widened as if he'd just been asked the stupidest question in the world. Then he turned to the class. "You all know what are American names, don't you?"

Werner glanced around the room. Every student's face appeared frozen. No one raised their hand.

Mr. Pendergrast seemed disappointed. "Then I suppose I must tell you myself." He spoke very deliberately, listing each name. "James as in James Monroe is an American name. John as in John Adams is an American name; Paul as in Paul Revere, Alexander as in Alexander Hamilton, and Andrew as in Andrew Jackson. These are all good American names."

His voice grew louder and his eyes narrowed. "Werner is *not* an American name. There has never been a president or any great American named *Werner*." The corners of Mr. Pendergrast's mouth turned up in a grim smile. "And there *never* will be one. Don't you agree, class?"

Werner looked around again. All the students in the class were dumbly nodding their heads like marionettes on a string. He turned slowly, walked back to his desk, and sank into his seat. Above anything, he wanted to be a good American. Did he have the wrong name? Should he change his name?

Walking home after school with Sam, he asked, "Is Sam an American name?"

His friend shrugged. "I dunno for sure. But I think there wuz a president or some famous American named Sam."

That night, Werner slouched around doing the chores, barely speaking to Esther.

"What's the matter, dearie?"

He looked at Esther without answering. He knew Mr. Pendergrast would hate the name Esther. American ladies were named Mary or Martha or Abigail or Alice. They were not named Esther. As for her being crippled, the teacher had already told the class about polio.

"Polio was brought to America by foreigners, immigrants," he had announced. "They infected the water in our swimming pools and lakes. Now it's dangerous to go in the water."

Mr. Pendergrast had stared directly at Werner. "This horrid foreign disease has struck down our own American president, Franklin Roosevelt. He was a wealthy man, too, from one of the best families in this country." He had shaken his head sadly, as if the germs must have made a big mistake. Then he glanced around the room, eyeing every student as if one of them might be responsible for the president's illness.

Werner had also looked around the room. What seemed odd to him was that not one student in Mr. Pendergrast's classroom was named James or John. The boys in the class had names like Reuben, Emmanuel, José, and Hector. The girls were Tanya, Sadie, and Hannah. He figured that's why Mr. Pendergrast appeared so very unhappy. He didn't have one genuinely American child in his class.

Though he clearly didn't like Werner, Mr. Pendergrast kept him in his fourth grade as long as possible. Even when the boy knew more than any other student.

"He keeps you in his class because he likes to torture you," said Sam.

"Torture? What does that mean?" Werner asked.

"Don't you remember the movie *King Kong*?" Sam asked. The two boys occasionally slipped into the exit of movie theaters when there was a really terrific film playing, like *King Kong* or *Tarzan*. "That huge gorilla gets picked on so much, he goes crazy and starts killing people."

Werner nodded. He pictured King Kong on top of the

Empire State Building, grabbing at airplanes. He felt soon he
might become as desperate as King Kong. Finally, he spoke to
Mrs. McIntosh. At first, she told him to be patient. "It's possible to learn from every sort of person, every kind of teacher."

"But Mrs. McIntosh, he hates me," Werner pleaded. "And
I think he hates almost every pupil in the class." Then Werner
told her what Mr. Pendergrast had said about polio and about
his name. Aghast, she told the principal, and Mr. Stromboski
was shocked, for he insisted that Mr. Pendergrast let Werner
move on to the fifth grade.

As Werner picked up his pencils and other supplies to leave
the room, Mr. Pendergrast glared at him. Gosh, he thought,
I feel sorry for the kids who are stuck here for the rest of the
year.

Werner still spent every lunch hour with Mrs. McIntosh.
Sometimes they worked on math or English or social studies.
Sometimes they just talked.

"Imagine the most wonderful place you've ever seen. There
are thousands of trees, acres and acres of grass, several ponds, a
zoo, and a lake." That's how Mrs. McIntosh described Central
Park to Werner. She and Mr. McIntosh and his eighty-year-old
mother visited there every Sunday afternoon.

Living so far downtown, Werner and Sam had never
thought of going to Central Park. They could get there on
the subway, of course, but it was a big trip. In fact, Werner
wouldn't ever have thought of going except for Julius....

What happened was that one warm Saturday afternoon in
early April, Werner had carried Julius downstairs to the street.
He figured the turtle would enjoy the fine weather out of his
crate. As soon as he put Julius on the pavement, the little crit-
ter stuck out his head and looked around. He had only two
tiny holes for a nose, but he could smell garbage. Apple cores,
chewing gum, orange peels, candy wrappers – whatever was lit-
tering the pavement. He darted after everything he could find.

In a few minutes, a crowd of kids had gathered around the

little turtle. To Julius, it must have seemed like a wall of feet. He stopped sniffing, tucked himself back inside his shell, and wouldn't come out again that day. Werner sadly carried his crate back to the apartment, telling Sam, "Julius needs grass."

"Grass?" said Sam. "Where we gonna find grass for Julius?"

Werner thought and thought, then a beautiful image appeared to him. "I know where there's a sea of grass," he announced.

Sam's eyes rolled. "A sea of grass? Are you kidding? You gotta go all the way to New Jersey to find a sea of grass."

That's when Werner suggested the two of them make a trip to Central Park next Saturday when the grocery store was closed. Werner worked every other day, carefully putting away the pennies, nickels, and dimes he earned for the day when Father and Bettina would arrive. Now he had something else to look forward to – Central Park!

Chapter Eighteen

When the day arrived for their big excursion uptown, Werner awoke early and glanced over. Esther was still asleep. A soft smile played on her lips; her greying hair was spread out on the pillow like a thin veil. He opened the window and stuck out his hand to check the weather. The air was mild, not too cool or too warm. Above he could see a stripe of blue sky. The sunshine already seemed bright enough to chase any clouds away.

Werner lifted Julius out of his crate and stuck him in a brown paper bag. "Today's your big day, little fella."

"You gonna be gone for a while, Werner?" called Esther, her eyelids fluttering as she awoke.

He tucked the bag under his light jacket. "Yeah, for a few hours. You want some tea? I can fix you some real quick."

Esther smiled. "Don't worry, I can already tell I'm gonna have a good day. I'll be out of bed soon and around the apartment on my own. You go ahead, Werner. I know you're planning some fun. Take off, enjoy yourself."

Barely ten minutes later he joined Sam on the street, and the two headed for the nearest subway station. They followed the crowd down the stairs to the platform. Soon the train rumbled into the station, screeching loudly as it stopped. Werner covered his ears to block out the noise. Nobody else even seemed to notice. Everyone pushed onto the subway car. Jostled by the crowd, Werner gripped the paper bag with Julius in it tight to his chest. "Don't worry," he muttered to the turtle. "It's gonna be a great day."

The subway tore down a long dark tunnel, whizzing past

everything outside the windows. Werner tried to read the signs on the stations, but they leapt into view and then disappeared. Finally Sam elbowed him. "Here's where we get off."

Dozens of people tumbled off the train. They all seemed to know where they were going, and everyone was in a hurry. Sam and Werner headed toward the exit and rushed up the stairs. Central Park was straight ahead.

Stepping into the sunlight outside the subway station, however, Werner stopped short. Was he still in New York City? Nothing he saw resembled anything he'd seen before. The buildings, the cars, even the people seemed taller and grander. Every car spinning by was a shiny limousine or a bright new yellow taxi. And there were lots of taxicabs, hundreds. Why, people who lived here, Werner thought, could hail a cab anytime they wished.

Sam's eyes were just as wide. A moment later, however, he started to saunter across the street with a "What's the big deal?" expression on his face.

Halfway across the avenue, however, the boys started running like robbers. They couldn't help themselves. The smell of green lured them like hot bread from a bakery lures a starving man. Ahead of them was the soft spring green of trees, bushes, and grass for as far as they could see. The minute their feet hit the park, they paused to look around. They weren't the only folks eager to enjoy Saturday at Central Park. The paths swarmed with well-dressed people. Some gripped leashes, pulling or being pulled by dogs. Not skinny, mangy dogs like the ones living downtown. These fat hounds had shiny black noses pointing high in the air.

Werner kept his feet on the gravel path for a short while. But his whole body yearned to feel earth beneath him. He ran off the path and plopped down with his belly flat on the ground. He spread out his arms and lay his cheek on the cool blades of grass.

"Whatcha doin'?" Sam grinned and pointed to a sign:

"KEEP OFF THE GRASS."

Werner lifted his head, then let it drop. "So what?" he muttered.

So what if a police officer showed up and told him to move? He wasn't afraid of cops. Not anymore. Not here in America. Here the cops were fair and honest and helpful. That's what Esther always told him.

A moment later, Werner sat up and opened the paper bag. His eyes brightened as he lifted Julius out of the bag, just imagining the joy in store for the little creature. The turtle's head and feet immediately popped out from beneath his shell. Werner carefully put him down in the grass. No sooner did Julius's tiny paws hit the ground, then he was flat-out running.

Sam laughed. "Jeepers, look at him go! He's a racing turtle!"

Alarmed, Werner jumped up and dashed after Julius. He feared the turtle would disappear deep into the bushes. Sure enough, a minute later, the little guy was out of sight. Werner scrambled under the low branches of a bush.

It was damp and muddy beneath the bush, but Werner kept crawling. Finally he grabbed Julius and climbed out, gripping the turtle.

"Gosh, Sam, he nearly got away." Werner looked worried. "Maybe I should put him back in the bag for a while."

Sam scratched his head a moment; a tiny frown appeared between his thick black eyebrows. "That's what you wanna do, Werner? Keep him in a bag all day?"

"Of course not," Werner said. "It's just...it's just we'll have to watch him real close and not let him get away."

Sam glanced around at the big trees, the bushes and the sea of grass.

"You *like* being watched real close, Werner?"

Hearing Sam's words, a tightness seized his chest. "What do you mean?"

His friend shrugged. "It just seems like Julius is real suited to this park."

Werner's lower lip stuck out a bit. "What of it, Sam? I like the park too." He glanced around. That sure was an understatement. He'd only been there ten minutes and already Central Park topped the list of places he liked to be.

"You'd stay here if you could, wouldn't you?" said Sam.

Werner shrugged. "I don't like it *that* much."

"Even if you was a turtle?" Sam eyed him carefully.

Werner didn't speak. Not ten feet away, a squirrel sat upright, its bright little eyes watching their every move. Overhead the pale green April leaves trembled in a breeze. A hundred yellow daffodils waved gracefully in a patch nearby. Werner caught a whiff of their fresh scent.

No doubt about it, Central Park was fantastic. For boys, for girls, for turtles, birds, squirrels, for any living creature. An idea slowly formed in Werner's head like jello thickening in the icebox. "You think Julius doesn't want to…. that he doesn't want to …" He could barely mouth the words. "You think he doesn't want to come back with us?"

Sam looked down and studied the ground. He didn't say anything. He didn't have to because Werner knew what he was thinking. *Why would Julius want to live in a smelly old crate when he could live here? In this great green garden of a place?*

Sam was right, entirely right. Still, Werner's chest felt so tight, it was hard to breathe. Maybe he felt a little jealous. Every day Julius was going to enjoy flowers, trees, bushes, and other small animals, while soon Sam and Werner would have to head back downtown. They'd have to return to concrete sidewalks, noisy streets, and stuffy little rooms. Yet Werner knew he couldn't complain. His life in the United States was free in ways he had never guessed were possible. He was incredibly lucky to be where he was – *Julius should be that lucky, too.*

Once out of the bag, the little turtle zipped off through the grass. The boys watched him go. "Why, it's like he knows just where he's going," exclaimed Sam. "Like he's been here before."

"Maybe he has been here," murmured Werner. "Maybe he

got lost and that's how he ended up in our neighborhood." He watched the turtle disappear, then flicked some grass off his shirt. The tightness in his chest had loosened.

"Hey, I'll race you!" he shouted to Sam and took off running. He felt his chest expanding as it filled with clear, clean air. Sam and he chased one another down one path and up another. Unlike the rest of the city that was mostly flat, the park was filled with grassy knolls and rocky summits. Sam scrambled up the slope of a hill, lay flat, and rolled back down. "Now you do it, Werner," he dared.

Werner's eyes widened – he'd never done such a thing in his life, but, golly, it looked like fun! Lying down, he stretched out full-length. Thick, cool grass tickled his neck and face. He hesitated a second, then turned over and over down the hill, going faster and faster with the blue sky whirling above. In that instant, he felt wild, crazy, and free, so free!

At the bottom of the hill, Werner lay for a moment, dizzy and happy. Then he stood up, and the two boys laughed hard.

"What should we do next?" Werner shouted. His friend shrugged, and they both started running, with no care where they were heading. In a minute they had reached the crest of another hill. Looking down they spotted a large oval pool of water, wide and smooth. In the center was a single sail, a white triangle, gliding across the water like it was on a mysterious voyage. For a long moment the boys just stared, then they raced down the hill to the edge of the pool.

The sailboat belonged to a little boy. He was using a long pole to keep his boat from bumping into others. He guided the little boat back and forth across the water. Several old men in sweaters and caps stood watching. Followed the ship's little voyage, neither Sam nor Werner noticed the reflection of grey clouds scooting across the pond's smooth surface.

A moment later, however, drops of rain began sharply pinging the water, and the boys' faces. The child quickly pulled his boat from the water and tucked it under one arm. He and the old men moved down the path. The rain was falling hard now. People rushed in every direction. Some had umbrellas, which they sprang open. Everyone was leaving the park in a hurry.

Sam turned to Werner. "Should we head home?"

"Leave now?" Werner shook his head. What was a little rain? "Not me."

Suddenly the sky opened up. Buckets of water dropped on their heads. Their clothes became so wet they could have been swimming in the pond, instead of gazing at it. The sunny warmth gave way to a chill that cut through their thin shirts. "We better run for it!" Sam shouted.

The two ducked under the branches of a big oak tree, but its mantle of new leaves didn't protect them for long. They took off toward a gazebo and cowered under its roof for several minutes. But the gazebo was open on all sides and the wind whipped the rain through it. "This isn't any good." Werner yelled and began running down a path that seemed to lead out of the park.

Moments later, they stood on the edge of Central Park, gazing across a wide avenue. The downpour had slowed the traffic. Cabs and limousines crept along the street, honking loudly.

On the other side of the street, they spied a small crowd of people huddled beneath an awning. The awning covered the entrance to a large, fancy apartment building.

"Let's go for it!" Sam shouted, and they crossed the street, dodging between honking taxicabs.

In front of the building, however, a tall man in a grey uniform with gold braid and matching cap marched back and forth. Over his head, he held up a large black umbrella.

As the boys drew near, he yelled at them. "Where do you punks think you're going?!"

Sam and Werner swerved as if they were heading in another direction. But a second later, they sneaked under the wide awning, pressing close to the building, just out of sight they believed, from the doorman. Besides, the doorman was too busy helping people in and out of limousines to notice. The boys stuck close together, shivering. They were happy to be out of the storm, as thunder crashed and a bolt of lightning lit the sky in a bright glow.

That's when Werner spied Anika.

Months and months had passed, so he didn't recognize her immediately. He watched as a thin, dark-haired girl climbed out of a limousine and walked toward the building. The color of her coat, however, caught his eye. It was purple with a little black fur collar. But the coat now seemed a bit faded and worn, and the collar lacked its sheen. Werner looked closer at the girl. It was Anika, all right. Her pale skin, dark eyes, and curly hair stood out clearly. As always, her head was held high with her jaw firmly set.

But he also glimpsed something unhappy in her face. Her eyes didn't sparkle; her mouth was pinched in a tight line.

Werner wondered what could be wrong. Her clothes were still fine, and she didn't look starved. And best of all, she lived right across the street from Central Park. Here she was, near one of the greatest places in the city, a place she could visit any day of the week, any time of day. So why was she unhappy?

Werner stepped closer, calling softly, "Anika."

Her head turned.

He knew the instant she spotted him. There was a quick gasp of surprise and a flash of happiness. She opened her mouth, then shut it quickly. Her lovely face closed like when a shade has been pulled down over a window. She lifted her chin high, looked straight ahead and marched on.

Then Werner saw what might be the problem. A chubby girl and boy with frizzy carrot-colored hair followed Anika from the limousine. The twins were both wearing brand new clothes. In fact, they carried heavy shopping bags, like they'd just come from a big buying spree at a department store. The looks on their faces, however, were not so nice. Their round freckled faces were conceited and unfriendly.

The big doorman ignored Anika, but tipped his cap to the other two. "Hallo there, Master Furstburner. Don't you look spiffy today, Miss Furstburner!"

"Thanks, Rudolf," the boy said loudly. He tossed a shiny coin to the doorman, glancing around to make sure people noticed what a big shot he was. His sister gave a prissy little smirk.

Werner shook his head. Poor Anika. After being forced to leave her beloved father, she deserved a good family, someone like his own dear Esther. Not these stuck-up kids.

The carrot tops and Anika disappeared behind a glass door that circled round and round.

"Now I gotta come back," Werner muttered to himself. He wanted to see Central Park again, of course, but he also wanted to see Anika. He wanted to cheer up his lively, fun-loving friend. At least now he knew where she lived.

"Whatcha sneaking round here for!" shouted the doorman, spotting the two boys. He rushed over and gave Sam such a hard push, he nearly ended up flat on the pavement. The two didn't delay. In a few seconds, they'd run halfway down the block.

Rudolf was still yelling, "You scum! Don't ever come back!"

The rain let up a bit as the boys dashed back to the subway. They pushed through the crowds, then Sam leapt over the turnstile and Werner followed. What an amazing day it had been!

While waiting for the train, Sam quizzed his friend. "So who was she?"

"Who was who?" Werner said, staring at the tracks.

"Your *girl*, that's who," he replied.

"She's *not* my girl."

"Oh, no?" said Sam with a sly grin.

Chapter Nineteen

As soon as Werner returned from Central Park, he discovered something was very wrong. The apartment was dark and cold. He could barely see Esther. When he called her name, he found the poor woman in bed covered with blankets.

Oh my God. He glanced across the room. The window was half open. His mind darted back to that morning. He'd been so excited about the trip that he'd opened it when he checked the weather. And then he'd left it open. That had seemed fine at the time, but now he recalled the sudden rainstorm that had drenched Sam and him in Central Park. The storm had quickly pushed away the spring sunshine, pelting them with rain and chilling the air with gusts of wind. The same storm must have visited here. The radiators had been turned off a month ago. The apartment could easily turn cold and drafty.

Werner rushed across the room and slammed down the window – though he knew it was too late.

"Thanks, Werner," murmured Esther from beneath the covers. "I meant to get up and do that myself. Just didn't get 'round to it." Her voice was weak.

"Esther, I'm so very..." he mumbled.

"Don't you worry, Werner," she added. "I just hope you and Sam had a good time. And how's the little guy, what's his name, your turtle?"

Werner felt a pang in his heart. A cold dark apartment and an empty crate, not much to cheer him up.

"Maybe later you can head down to Mr. Mozer's," said Esther. "I wouldn't mind reading the news."

Werner barely heard her. He cranked open a can of

mushroom soup and poured it into a pot. "The news, the news – why have you always gotta read the news?" He banged the soup pot down on the burner. "You oughta quit reading the dumb news! It makes you so miserable."

Esther was silent a moment. "It's worse *not* knowing, isn't it, *bubele*?" she murmured. "And if you don't know what's going on, how can you do anything?"

"Do anything? What difference does it make what we do?" Werner muttered. "The Nazis are winning! They're beating everybody!"

He poured Esther a bowl of soup and brought it to her on a tray, then hurried downstairs to the grocery. He felt terrible about the drafty cold apartment. All day he'd been having a swell time. All day he'd forgotten about the news, the war in Europe, Father and Bettina, and Esther.

What he'd just said, however, was true. By late spring, Nazi Germany had gobbled up Czechoslovakia, Poland, Denmark, Norway, Belgium, Luxembourg, and Holland. The map of Europe looked like a bottle of black ink had toppled over and drenched the continent with dark blotches. Only brave little England stood fast against the Nazi forces.

Every day newsboys on every street corner shouted out grim headlines like "Holland floods its own fields to stop Nazi advance! But nothing stops the Huns!"

When he reached Mr. Mozer's store that evening, he found the old man sitting on a stool behind the counter. After sundown on Saturday night, the grocery opened for a few hours. People who'd run out of eggs or bread on the Sabbath came by. It was also a time for people from the neighborhood to gather together and share news and opinions. Mr. Mozer sat on a stool behind the cash register while a few customers stood nearby.

"War's getting closer and closer every day," said Mr. Mozer. "I can smell it just around the corner."

"For Pete's sake, why should America get into another dirty war from Europe?" said Leo Zinitsky. "We lost plenty of good

Americans the last time. We'd be stupid to do it again."

"This ain't the same," said Emma Krohof. "The Nazis are bad people. They're killing Jews and communists and any decent person who stands up against 'em."

"What? You think it's worse now than the pogroms we faced thirty years ago in Russia?" asked Leo. "Ten, twenty, fifty Jews used to get killed every week! Ain't that why so many of us came here?" He glanced around the crowd.

"I can't see how anybody, even the damn Nazis, could murder people like we hear they're doing," said Aron Tishfelt. "It's propaganda – trying to get us angry so we'll sign up for another war. Not me, not this time, I ain't going."

"Don't go, Aron, if you don't want to, you chump! But I sure will!" exclaimed Himmel Kauffeldt. He was a young man who brought crates of brown farm eggs from Long Island every day. "I'll fight and fight until the Nazis are all dead."

Himmel and Aron looked ready to punch each other right that minute. With a weary look, Mr. Mozer turned to Werner, "You wuz there, kid. You come from Germany a short time ago. Wuz it so bad as they say?"

Everyone turned and stared at the boy. He wished he could slip between the cracks in the floor. How do you describe hunger to a person with a full belly? Or a storm at sea when the waves are calm? Who would believe the awful stuff? Yet he knew he needed to speak up. How else would people know what was happening?

"Is it so bad as they say?" Aron Tishfelt repeated.

Werner nodded, "It's worse. Much worse."

The little group fell silent. In their bones, many of them knew that the night in Europe was becoming blacker, especially for Jews. Yet what could anybody do about it? Only the American president, Franklin Roosevelt, could stand up against Nazi Germany. And to do that, he needed to gain the support of the U.S. Congress and the American people. According to the news, the president was slowly, steadily moving the United

States into the war on the side of England. Hurray for the president, thought Werner. If only he'd hurry up. President Roosevelt needed to move as fast as the comic hero Superman to beat Adolf Hitler!

At that moment, Oscar Buddorf entered the little store and began buying groceries. He calmly put a hunk of Swiss cheese and a bottle of mustard into his cart. His yellowish teeth tightly clenched a pipe that issued a cloud of sweetish grey smoke.

Seeing Buddorf, the small group of Jewish customers fell into a gloomy silence. They eyed him tensely and didn't speak up until he left with a bag of groceries. Then Aron Tishfelt muttered, "That guy gives me the creeps."

"He ain't like other *krauts* in the neighborhood." Leo Zinitsky shook his head. "Like Mrs. Schultz that teaches kindergarten, or Mr. Heine that's a plumber. Buddorf's a real wacko."

"What is that group he belongs to? The German Bund?" Emma Krostof shuddered. "They're…they're un-American, that's what I think!"

"I don't know," said Mr. Mozer soberly. "There's more Americans think like he does than you ever wanna know."

Werner didn't have time to listen further. He grabbed the used newspapers from under the counter and ran back upstairs to look after Esther. She sounded like she might have gotten a cold in her chest. What if she got any sicker? It would be his fault, completely. And he knew who would be angrier than heck. Tomorrow Conrad would arrive at 3 p.m. exactly. What would he say? What might he do?

Dashing up the stairs, Werner prayed she'd be well by then.

Chapter Twenty

But Esther wasn't well the next day. Waking a few times during the night, Werner heard her gasp for air. She sat nearly upright, propped on pillows, just trying to breathe in and out.

By Sunday morning she was exhausted.

"Tell Mr. Boronski and the others that I can't help today," she muttered wearily. "I'm so sorry. Maybe later this week." Werner bent close to hear her voice.

"Now, you gotta take care of yourself now, Esther," he insisted, feeding her spoonfuls of sweet hot tea. "That's what's important."

"But we can't turn our backs on our neighbors and our relatives," she whispered to him.

Werner shrugged, yet he knew she was right. What if she'd turned her back on him and his family? Where would he be now?

"You want me to cut your hair, Werner?" Esther murmured. "I haven't done it in a while." The boy shook his head. Just like her to be thinking of him when she was feeling so low.

A little later Esther started coughing. Coughing and coughing. Flecks of blood hit the pillow around her. Werner carefully lifted her head and put a clean towel beneath it. He anxiously watched the clock as the hours ticked by – 12 p.m...1 p.m...2 p.m...2:50 p.m. He paced back and forth in the tiny space. Conrad would be arriving any minute.

"I'm going downstairs to see Mr. Mozer," he said to Esther.

She barely nodded; she didn't look good. Paler than usual, she hadn't put on lipstick and brushed her hair as she usually did for Conrad's visits. She still struggled to catch every breath.

Werner passed Conrad on the stairs. In a hurry as usual, the short man didn't glance over. He didn't yet know.

Twenty minutes later, however, Werner stood in front of the grocery store, tossing a ball with Sam. Conrad marched up. His face was beaded with sweat. He looked like steam might spew out of his ears any second.

Glaring at Sam, he muttered, "Why don't you get lost for a few minutes!"

Sam glanced at Werner, who nodded okay. His friend walked slowly away, whistling.

Conrad didn't waste any time. "Hey, wise guy, you notice somebody who's not feeling so good?"

"Esther's not feeling well." Werner stared at the pavement beneath his feet.

"You figured that out, did ya?" Conrad's voice seethed with anger. "She was doing fine a week ago. How come she's so sick right now?"

"Sh-she didn't tell you?" Werner stammered.

"Nah, but I'd bet ten bucks you know what happened and twenty you're the person responsible!" Conrad wagged his finger in the boy's face. "You being stupid or lazy. Or both!"

Werner didn't answer. What could he say? Conrad was right – he had been stupid and careless. He'd been thinking of his trip uptown, of Julius and beautiful Central Park. He hadn't been thinking of Esther.

Conrad wasn't interested in an answer anyway; he got right to the point. "She's too sick to stay on her own up there," he muttered, glancing toward the fourth floor window. "She needs somebody who can really take care of her."

Werner's heart flipped. Was Conrad going to take Esther away? For how long – a week, a month? Would he ever see her again?

"Where will she go?" he asked.

"There's a special hospital for people with her kinda disease. I'm gonna take her there," Conrad said.

"N-now?" Werner stammered.

"Tomorrow. Soon as I can put the money together." Conrad glared at him. "Doctors don't come cheap, you know? You been soaking up all her extra cash for months. But that's finished now. You're finished now." His face turned hard. "Get her things ready to go. I'll be back for her tomorrow, you hear?"

He whirled around and started down the street, then turned back. "And don't think you can hang out here forever on your own. No, siree. Not you, not if you got nothing to do!"

As soon as Conrad took off, Sam returned. "You okay, pal?" He tossed the ball at him but Werner didn't catch it. It bounced down the sidewalk as he headed toward the apartment. "I got a lot to do."

That evening, he spent every moment tending to Esther. He brought her cups of hot chicken broth, sitting on the bed and spooning the soup to her lips. He read pieces of the newspaper aloud, though some of it was old news.

"You're so good to me, Werner." Esther reached up and ruffled his hair gently. He looked away; his stomach was starting to ache badly. "What's the matter, sweetie?" she added. "Anything wrong?"

"Nothing's the matter, Esther, I promise," Werner replied. "Please don't worry."

It was enough for him to worry. He fought off the vision of holding his mother's hand for the last time. This can't be, he thought. This can't happen to me again...it can't.

That evening, when Esther fell asleep, he gathered up her sweaters, socks, and underwear. He put them in a little grey suitcase from the closet. He had to clear away a few cobwebs, since it hadn't been used in years.

Werner glanced around. There wasn't much else to do. Not now. His face felt tight, like a thin coat of paint had been brushed across it. He sat on the edge of his bed and glanced through his old comic books, but the stories didn't draw him in. Then he picked up a shabby U.S. geography textbook that

Mrs. McIntosh had given him. Werner had thumbed through it again and again, eager to know what the whole country looked like. Now he flipped through the pages. There were pictures of neighborhoods with rows of neat little houses and green lawns. There were farms with red barns and fat cows. But his favorite section was "The West." He loved the pictures of cowboys roping steers, of Indians on horseback, of mountains, prairies, and deserts. The West looked open and free. Just like Alf's stories.

Werner's head finally dropped to his pillow. Dreams of coyotes and grizzly bears spun in his brain.

"Open up! You hear me?"

Conrad was yelling and pounding on the door. It was morning already. He entered with two big men and a stretcher.

"You got her clothes?" he demanded.

Werner handed him the little grey suitcase. The two strong guys slowly lifted Esther onto the stretcher. "Careful now. You be careful." Conrad's face was stiff with worry. She lay on the stretcher limply, barely breathing, only half-awake.

Conrad followed the men down the stairs. Werner watched through the window as Esther was carefully loaded into an ambulance on the street. It seemed like half the neighborhood was watching as well.

Barely a minute later, Conrad returned, shut the door and walked straight toward Werner. Though only forty, he looked eighty. His head was sunk in his shoulders, and he gazed at the boy with a hard, unforgiving stare.

"You know it's your fault! You lousy *nogoodnik*." He jabbed his stubby fingers into the boy's chest. "You had a job to do and you didn't do it, did ya!" He poked at Werner again. "Whatcha thinks gonna happen now? What's gonna happen to my darlin' Esther?"

The man's face was creased with pain. His hands curled into fists and he struck several sharp punches at Werner, right and left. Werner stepped back, trying to get clear, but not fast enough. Conrad socked him right below the chest; Werner gasped for breath. Then Conrad peppered him again and again with hard jabs.

Werner ducked the blows, at first, but didn't fight back. After all, he figured, *Conrad was right.* It was his fault that Esther got sick. He'd goofed up bad; he deserved whatever punishment he got.

But then Conrad's fists became hammers, knocking him from side to side. He struck the boy's face, busting open his lip and bruising his cheek. From Conrad's face, Werner saw that the man was blind with anger. He wasn't just going to punish the boy, he was going to kill him....He would kill him!

That's when Werner raised his fists and began fighting back. He was taller than Conrad, though not as strong. The man knocked him down, but Werner grabbed his shirt and pulled him down, too. The two rolled on the floor, striking and kicking each other. Conrad managed to get on top and slammed the boy's head against the floor. Once, twice, three times. Werner felt dizzy. In another second, he'd pass out, and if Conrad kept punching him, he'd soon be dead. With all his strength, Werner jabbed a knee hard into Conrad's gut, pushed him off, and rolled away.

He readied himself for another attack. But it didn't come. For some reason Conrad didn't keep slugging. He lay still for several moments while the fight drained out of him. Then he rolled over and clambered up, grabbing the back of a chair for balance.

Werner remained on the floor another minute, dabbing the blood on his face with his finger.

Gripping the chair, Conrad stared down at the boy. When he spoke, it sounded like each word was pulled from deep inside. "You don't understand, do you kid?" Tears ran down his cheeks. "We had it all lined up, Esther and me. Ever since she got to this country, ever since we first met. Maybe she was nine, maybe I was ten, but it was always just her and me. Me and her." His shoulders slumped. "We wuz sweethearts."

Conrad stared beyond Werner as if he wasn't speaking to the boy. He was addressing the Fates that had ruled his life. That had dumped on him. "Nothing wuz gonna get in our way. Not her folks, not my folks, not nuttin'." Again, he pulled the words from a long buried place. "Then this…this disease, it came along…a week or two before our wedding date. It came along and destroyed every chance we had. Every chance we had for a beautiful life together. The two of us, always together."

"You mean the polio?" Werner murmured.

"Whatcha know about polio?" Conrad snarled and his fingers curled into fists again. "It's a mean disease, a cruel disease. It don't always kill you right away but it can ruin you." His fingers uncurled and his hands dropped to his sides. It was obvious he didn't want to fight anymore. "I says to Esther, "Marry me anyway," but she won't do it. She couldn't have children, she said, so she wouldn't be a real wife. "I want you to have a family, Conrad. I want you to have your own sons and daughters."" His chin dropped to his chest. "Like *that's* what I wanted."

"Do you?" Werner asked, climbing unsteadily off the floor. "Do you have a family?"

"Sure." His head jerked up. "I married a gal named Trudy, a real big gal, bigger than me, and we have three kids. *Brats*, I call 'em. Still, I pay the rent and put food on the table." His jaw jutted out proudly. "But that ain't stopped me from showing up here every Sunday, now has it? Every Sunday of the year!"

Conrad's eyes narrowed and a noise like a growl came from his throat. "You had a job to do and you didn't do it. In this country, you only get one chance. You hear? One chance! So if she…if something bad happens to Esther…." He shot Werner another hard look, then staggered toward the door, calling back as he left. "You're in trouble. Big trouble!"

Werner heard him stumble once or twice going down the stairs, but he kept going.

Seconds later, the boy collapsed onto his cot. He felt like one of the delivery trucks on Second Avenue had slammed smack into him. Every cell in his body hurt. Yet he wasn't dead. Conrad had used him for a punching bag – the man had struck out against everything in his life that hadn't gone right – but he hadn't killed Werner. Not yet.

Still, what would happen if Esther didn't get well? What would Conrad do then? Kick him out of the apartment? Send him back to Germany?

She just *had* to get well.

Meanwhile, Werner realized, he needed a plan. If forced to, he could survive on the streets like his friend Alf. But that was just him. What about Father and Bettina? They might arrive soon. They needed a safe place to live, and food to eat. From the letters he'd written, Father would assume both were available. What could Werner write to them now? He didn't dare write the truth, because that might delay their coming. So what could he tell them?

These thoughts whirled round and round Werner's brain until his head dropped to the pillow. He dozed uneasily. In his dream, a monstrous person was chasing him through a winding maze. He tried hard to escape but couldn't find a way out. And the monster's face kept changing. First it was Eckhard, the sailor on the ship, ready to toss him to the sharks. Then it was Mr. Pendergrast, jabbing at him with an American flag attached to a sharp flagpole. The monster dissolved into Rudolf chasing him and calling him "scum." Finally, the monster's face was Oscar Buddorf with grey smoke spewing from his pipe.

When Werner awoke, hours later, the room felt cold and *empty*. Esther had filled it with warm kindness. Now that she was gone, what was left? He looked around slowly. Only Mozart remained – that fluffy ball of yellow feathers. Poor bird – Werner had forgotten to take the cover off his cage. Did the tiny bird think it was still night? As soon as Werner removed the cover, the canary lifted its tiny beak and began to sing. Its brave little song filled the empty room.

A moment later, a familiar footstep sounded on the stairs, and Sam bounded through the door. From his expression, Werner could see that his pal knew about Esther. News traveled fast in that neighborhood, especially bad news. He flinched, however, when he saw Werner's bruised face. "You don't look so good, bud. What'd you do, walk into a door?"

Werner groaned, pouring out his worries. "What am I gonna do, Sam?"

His friend shrugged. "We'll think of something, buddy." Sam glanced around the little apartment. "Whatcha got to eat? A person can always think better on a full stomach, that's what Ma says."

Werner opened a can of soup, and the two finished off all the milk, cheese, peanut butter and crackers in the apartment. They still had no ideas.

"Wanna play checkers?" Sam suggested. He pulled the board from under the bed and chose red as usual.

Werner gazed across the checkerboard at his friend. Sam was studying the board for his next move. Some guys, he figured, are naturally nice. Not because their lives are *easier* – Sam's certainly wasn't – but because they don't let the bad times ruin their hearts.

A few hours later, Sam took off for home. First though, he patted Werner's arm. "I promise, if we keep thinking, we'll figure something out."

Werner was alone once more. But he didn't feel quite so bad. As long as you had one chum, he guessed, you could keep going.

Chapter Twenty-One

10 June, 1940

Dear Father,

   Amazing things happen in this country. Even to a kid like Sam. Yesterday, my friend came up to my room with his eyes big as saucers. "So whatcha think we should do today?" he asked. I didn't know what to say. It seemed like an ordinary day to me. But, anyway, Sam answered his own question. "We're going to Coney Island, that's what we're gonna do today!"

   Of course I didn't believe him. Every kid in the neighborhood wants to go to Coney Island. It's the greatest amusement park in the country, probably in the whole world. But we don't have the cash to go. It costs a lot.

   Then Sam explains that an hour ago, he was walking down the street, doing nothing special, when something green flew in front of him. When he went to see what it was, there was a crisp new $5 bill lying on the curb.

   Of course he didn't believe it was real at first. How could a real $5 bill just fly through the air? So he showed it to Mr. Mozer, who has seen hundreds of $5 bills. Mr. Mozer looked at it real close and said the money looked as good as any $5 bill he'd ever seen.

That's when Sam came to see me. He told me we could go to Coney Island on the train. Then he said, "And we're going today."

I asked Mr. Mozer and he said I could have a day off because I worked so hard every other day. So two hours later, we're there!!

First, we see the Cyclone – a huge rollercoaster with little wooden carts that go way up high...and then come crashing down. The riders were screaming their heads off. The man selling tickets tried to get us on board: "Twenty-five cents for the ride of a lifetime." Sam wanted to go, but not me. I asked Sam, "Have you ever been so scared you peed in your pants?" He shook his head. So I said, "Well, fear is a bad feeling, the worst in the world. Not something to pay 25 cents for."

So we walked and walked and looked and looked. We saw brass bands and Hawaiian hula dancers. We saw a dancing bear in a little purple hat and two monkeys in gold vests. We rode on a miniature railroad train that circled on its own little track.

A big guy with red whiskers talked Sam into playing a game like stickball. He just had to throw a ball into a hole about 15 feet away. Sam's a good stickball player and he spent over a dollar, throwing and throwing until the ball finally went in. He wanted to win a doll for his sister's birthday. The doll looked very pretty on the shelf – like Bettina's precious Minnie. But up close, dear sister, it wasn't near as pretty as your doll! Sam said his sister wouldn't care 'cause she'd never had a doll.

Finally we came to the best ride at Coney Island. It's called the Steeplechase and it's like a real racetrack. Except it has wooden horses instead of real horses. You ride the horses around the racetrack and try to grab a gold ring. Whoever gets the ring wins ten extra rides! We stood in line 40 minutes just to get on. I rode a black horse and Sam's horse was green. I was certain I could grab the ring. But it whizzed past both Sam and me.

Still, we had a dollar and a half to spend so we were looking for stuff to spend it on. We passed a big tent with a poster out front for Wild Bill Hickok and his Wild West Show. Inside it said there were bucking broncos, long-horned steers, buffaloes, Indians, and cowboys. The picture sucked me right in and I begged Sam to buy tickets.

But he said, "Are you kidding? Wild Bill Hickok has been dead for 20 years. What a waste of money! Besides, I'm starving." So we spent most of the money on Nathan's Hots. That's what they call frankfurters, covered with mustard, slaw and fried onions. And we drank two orange sodas each.

Then we were heading home but Sam begged me again to ride the Cyclone. And I finally agreed. Sam dished out two quarters and we climbed on board. The attendant slammed a metal bar across our knees to keep us in our seats. Then the little car climbed up and up and up. At the top, it paused a few seconds and I could see for miles all around. Every bit of Coney Island — the tents, the beach, the Atlantic Ocean. I thought about you and Bettina on the other side of the ocean. How I wished you were right here and not over there. Then the car started going down really fast...down, down, down, right to the bottom. Sam threw up his hot dogs and orange soda. On him and me. We tried to clean up but probably smelled bad on the train ride home.

I know this is a very, very long letter. But I wanted you to know about one of the great wonders of New York!

Love and kisses to you both,
Your son, Werner

Chapter Twenty-Two

Mailing his letter about Coney Island, Werner grinned. Father would be so pleased to find such a thick letter in their mailbox. He'd read it aloud to Bettina and she'd beg to hear it again and again. Both would be thrilled by his adventures!

Yet, even in this long letter, Werner hadn't described everything that had happened that day. For instance, he hadn't told Father *why* he had missed grabbing the gold ring on the Steeplechase ride....

The truth was that a few seconds before he had reached for the gold ring, he had spied a girl seated on a horse in front of him, a purple horse. The girl had a thin pale neck and dark curly hair. Werner had been so certain he knew who it was that he had called out loudly, "Anika!"

The girl on the purple horse had whipped around. She had a pug nose and glasses. She had frowned, then shouted. "Whatcha' yelling at me for? Ya stupid!" In that very second, the gold ring whizzed past. He'd missed his chance to reach for it.

That stupid mistake, however, reminded Werner that he did want to see Anika again, soon. She didn't live far across the ocean. She lived right in New York City. And he knew where.

But Anika wasn't the first person that Werner needed to see. The next day, Mr. Mozer gave him directions to the polio sanitarium where Conrad had taken Esther. It was about fifteen blocks away – a big old building, painted a dingy yellow. Werner brought a box of bright red cherries from the grocery store. He also carried Mozart in his cage.

The nurse in the front hall of the sanitarium nearly had a

fit. "You must be joking, kid. We don't let any animals in here."

"Mozart is not an animal," Werner explained. "He's a bird."

"Well, no birds either. They're dirty beasts."

At that moment, however, an elderly doctor came by. "Whatcha got there, young man?"

Werner explained that Mozart was the darling of Esther's life. "She will be so happy to see him."

"We can't let that bird in here!" said the crabby nurse.

The doctor looked thoughtful. "Music is good for sick people. And the people convalescing in here need all the help they can get."

"Honestly, Dr. Swenn, isn't that going a bit too far?" said the nurse. "A live bird!"

"It could hasten our patient's recovery."

"If you say so, Doctor." The nurse pursed her lips, but she didn't stop Werner from carrying Mozart upstairs.

He trudged up to the third floor where the polio ward for poor women was located. It was a long, wide room lined with beds. The beds were filled with women of all ages and colors – white, black, brown, and yellow.

Werner carefully placed Mozart's cage on a wide windowsill near Esther's bed. She was delighted to see her tiny friend. "Oh my God, Werner, how *wunderbar*! Now I really do feel good."

Despite her cheery tone, Esther looked as pale as the cotton sheet covering her thin body. She could barely raise herself from the bed to give him a hug. "I had pneumonia when I first came here," she explained, "but now I'm much better."

Werner wasn't so sure. Sitting on the edge of her bed, he handed her one cherry at a time. She delighted in each one. "So will you be coming home soon?" he asked in a low voice.

Esther's blue eyes clouded, and she sighed gently. "Maybe not soon, but some day...."

Then her eyes brightened. "How is Sam?" she asked. "How's Mr. Mozer and Mr. Boronski? I miss people so much."

"They're all fine," Werner assured her and then told her

about going to Coney Island. "Did you ever go?"

"Oh yes, Conrad and I went often before I got sick," Esther exclaimed. "He loved Coney Island and I liked it for his sake."

Werner nodded. He didn't like to be reminded of the short man with brown tufts of hair. He glanced around, hoping Conrad wouldn't show up that minute.

Even their short conversation seemed to tire Esther. She slid lower in the bed and a passing nurse motioned to Werner. He placed the rest of the box of cherries on a table next to the bed, then stood at the end of the bed and said a little prayer:

Please, God, I know how many people you must care for now. Millions of people all over the world. But please save a little time for Esther. She is such a special dear person.

He figured God must already know that. But it didn't hurt to remind Him.

Walking down the wide steps of the sanitarium, Werner's head hung low, thinking about how far he had traveled to find a safe home for himself and his family. But now the goal seemed further away than ever. Glancing around, the city suddenly appeared dirty, noisy, and crowded. What was so great about New York? If Father, Bettina, and he didn't have a good home here, why not go someplace else? Someplace completely different. His imagination soared – suddenly the tall buildings on either side melted into high jagged mountains while the traffic-clogged street seemed like a river torrent. Why not travel out West? Why not find a home amid the wide open plains, deserts and mountains? Some place clean and free. He could picture himself with Father and Bettina riding horses across the prairie, swimming in clear lakes, living in a mountain cabin.

The notion quickened Werner's steps. He ran all the way back to Second Avenue, his head filled with dreams.

And yet there was one thing he still wanted to do in the city. Something that wouldn't wait any longer. First, however, he had to convince Sam to go with him. He needed his friend's help for his plan to work.

Chapter Twenty-Three

It wasn't hard to find Sam now that school was out. He was playing stickball in a nearby empty lot. Werner quickly explained his idea. "Here's what you gotta do," he added, "you're gonna distract that stupid doorman Rudolf. Once his back is turned, I can slip inside."

Sam's eyebrows shot up. "Gee whiz, you're more of a goner than I thought."

"A goner? What does that mean?" said Werner.

"You're gone on that girl. What's her name? Anya…Anita?"

"I am not." Werner clenched his fists, ready to slug Sam if he spoke more nonsense.

"Okay, bud," he said quickly. "I'll go with you."

The next day the two got an early start. Both were looking forward to seeing Central Park again. It was hot now, and the trees, bushes, and grass would be greener than on their last trip.

"We might see Julius," exclaimed Werner.

"Are you kidding?" Sam looked disgusted. "That turtle's probably in Delaware by now."

The boys were talking so much they barely heard the voice that rang out from the apartment building high above. "Samuel Ublentz, I see you!" yelled a stout lady leaning out of a fifth-floor window. "You get up here now! Right this minute!"

Sam looked up, then shouted back, "Mom, I can't. Werner and I are heading uptown today."

"No, you're not," his mother replied. "I just got word your Uncle Rudy's broke his damn leg. I gotta take him to the doctor!" She jerked her thumb back toward the room. "And who's gonna watch these babies if you don't?"

Sam glanced at his pal. There was nothing to be done. When Sam's mother asked for something, you didn't say no. Werner halted a moment, unsure. His plan called for Sam's help. How could he do it on his own?

Sam started heading for home. "You'll figure something out, bud. You gotta go – for you and for her."

So, not ten minutes later, Werner was standing on a swaying subway train. He carefully watched as the stations flashed past. If he didn't get off at the right stop, there was no telling where he'd end up.

Arriving at Central Park, Werner felt once again like he was entering a different universe. People here were sharply dressed, their hair was shiny, and they smelled better, too.

A stylish blonde passed him on the sidewalk with a scent as sweet as flowers. She wore a green hat with a bouncy white feather. Werner trailed behind the lady, hypnotized by the feather. When she disappeared in the crowd, he settled down on a bench to watch. Old folks with quiet smiles shuffled along. Kids darted here and there. Young mothers pushed baby carriages with one hand, gripping toddlers with the other.

How lucky these folks were, he thought. They dwelled in a sparkly paradise. How could any of them imagine their good fortunes might be snatched away overnight? That they might be beaten or imprisoned? That they could suffer the fate of his family and Anika's and of a million other families in Europe?

Werner stood up and started to join the crowd when – *kaboom* – a plump little boy slammed into him and fell flat.

"Harry, Harry!" His mother rushed over. Frowning, she sized up Werner. "What are you doing here? You look like a bum." The woman grabbed Harry's hand and yanked the boy away. "Now, darling, I told you to stay clear of those people."

In an instant, Werner was snapped out of paradise. The rosy lens he'd been using to view people in this part of the city blurred. To them, he was a kid wearing hand-me-down clothes with a lousy haircut. A *nogoodnik*. Too bad Sam wasn't with him – his pal would have something choice to say to those snobs!

But what about Anika? Werner wondered suddenly. She might turn up her nose, too, when she saw him. Passing a public restroom, he anxiously ducked inside to inspect himself. In the mirror over a sink, he saw how much he'd changed in nine months. His face was fuller and had a much warmer color. His eyes looked bright and keen. His hair, however, was in terrible shape without Esther to clip it every week. So he splashed cold water on the shaggy mess, parted it on one side, then flattened it down as best he could.

He figured he looked as good as possible. Still, he was worried. Would Anika truly be happy to see him? He recalled the moment in the ship's corridor when she'd walked away without speaking. What if he showed up at the door and she pretended not to know him? How embarrassing that would be!

Werner stalled for a few minutes, unsure what to do. Finally, his feet made the decision. His steps turned him in the direction of Anika's building. He wanted to know why she looked so unhappy. Was it just those conceited twins? Or had she heard from her father? Was there any news? Werner needed to speak to her, even for one minute.

Since the day was sunny and clear, perhaps the doorman wasn't on duty. He might be able to walk inside, easy as pie. But Rudolf was standing out front, looking big, important, and puffed up as a Royal Guard for the Queen of England. He was whistling for taxis and helping people in and out of shiny black limousines. Werner observed him carefully. Rudolf's eyes roamed the sidewalk, scanning everyone who passed. It would not be easy to get past him.

After studying the situation for several minutes, however, Werner saw his chance. At the edge of the park, a balloon man was selling big red and blue balloons. A line of kids stood waiting to get theirs. One was a little girl with long yellow braids. She had come from Rudolf's apartment building with her pretty mother. After purchasing a blue balloon, the two headed back. The doorman was eyeing them both, especially the mother, with interest.

Choosing the right moment, Werner strolled past the child. Then he reached over and plucked the string from her hand. Let loose, the blue balloon sailed off. Stunned, the little girl started bawling. Everyone on the street turned to see, but nobody moved faster than Rudolf. He raced after the balloon, stretching his long arm up and reaching for the string. He had nearly grabbed the balloon when it soared skyward.

With Rudolf temporarily out of the way, Werner scrambled toward the door. Before rushing in, however, he glanced back. Sure enough, to please the unhappy child, Rudolf was standing in line to purchase another balloon.

Without wasting a second, Werner raced through the wide lobby. He nearly collided with a family of four in front of the elevator. Then he tried to blend in as they all waited patiently. When the door opened, the elevator operator eyed him suspiciously but said nothing. Asked his destination, Werner blurted out, "Furstburners, please." The elevator doors slid closed and the operator pressed the button marked 15th floor.

No one in the tight little space realized that Werner had never before been in an elevator. He gulped. What a funny sensation, almost like riding up on the Cyclone. He only hoped it didn't go down as fast. When the door at the 15th floor slid open, the operator peered at Werner. "Here you go, Furstburner residence."

Werner walked out, hoping he looked more confident than he felt. What if there were a dozen doors to choose from? Fortunately, there was one big grand door straight ahead with carved dark wood and a brass knocker in the shape of a lion. Beneath the lion was a gleaming plate that read: Nathan and Dorothy Furstburner.

Werner stared at the door with no idea what to do next. He could knock, of course. But what if the person who opened the

door took one look at him and slammed it in his face? Then
he'd never see Anika. He had to come up with a different plan.

Glancing around, Werner spied a small side door with the
sign "Ring for package delivery" and a little red button. Hurray! It was easy to pretend to be a grocery boy because he actu-
ally was a grocery boy. He just didn't have any groceries with
him. Still, it was the only plan he could think of. So he pressed
hard on the buzzer. A moment passed. Werner was ready to
press again when a mousy little maid in a black uniform with a
white apron opened the door. She stared at Werner.

"Who are you?" Her eyes were big and timid. "We weren't
expecting an order."

"I, *uh*, have a present for Anika from her father." Werner
kept his hands behind his back as if he was holding something.
"Is she here?"

The girl looked curious. "I can take it."

"N-no," Werner stammered. "Special instructions to give
it only to her." The maid stared at him another instant, then
turned back into the apartment.

A long minute passed. Werner forced himself to breathe
in and out slowly. He feared that the maid had gone to fetch
the Furstburners. They would know he was lying. They were
probably already calling the police. He started to turn from the
door, ready to dash away.

"*Werner?*"

Hearing her sweet thin voice, he swung back around. Anika
stood very still in a lacy white blouse and dark blue skirt. Next
to her, the maid was nudging her with an elbow. "I told you
somebody was here. You never believe me!"

The maid shrugged, then turned and left. Which is why she
didn't see what happened next.

Chapter Twenty-Four

Anika jumped into his arms. "*Werner, mein Werner,* thank goodness you've come!" She gave him a tight squeeze, then she pulled away, a radiant smile on her face.

His face was fire truck red and flaming hot, but only Anika could see, and she clearly didn't care.

"I am so happy you've come." Her eyes sparkled with tears. "I didn't think I'd ever see you again."

Werner's eyes fogged as well. His heart was thumping wildly.

"Why wouldn't I visit?" he mumbled. "Once I knew where you lived." He gazed at her closely. "I was worried."

"Worried?" Anika glanced at the big front door. A shadow crossed her face.

"Yeah, I could see you were unhappy," said Werner. "What's wrong?"

She hesitated, her lip trembling, then the words poured out. "It's the Furstburners, the family I live with. They're mean and selfish and never wanted me here in the first place."

"So why did they host you?"

She shrugged. "They're rich and proud. The rabbi at their synagogue begged people to take in 'the poor little children of Europe.'" Anika tossed her head proudly. How she hated to be pitied.

"Now they show me off to friends like a pet poodle with a gilt collar. Everyone *oohs* and *ahs* about how sad everything is in Germany. But they have no idea, do they?"

"What about the twins?" asked Werner, recalling the orange-haired duo.

"Norman and Nathalie? They're worse than their parents. They make fun of me. They say I'm old-fashioned." Anika mimicked Nathalie's voice: "No one wears velvet any more, not in America. We wear velveteen."

Anika took out a dainty lace hankie and wiped her eyes. "They make me play the piano, then say I'm stupid because I don't know American music."

She sniffed. "But I love Beethoven and Schumann. It's all I know how to play."

Her dark eyes widened. "Take me to *your* family. I'll live with them. I'm sure they're very nice. They won't mind. I promise I'll be sweet and helpful." She grabbed his hand. "Please, Werner, please, I hate it here!"

Werner gulped – how could he tell Anika that he didn't have a family? Not now. He barely had a place to live. And he might not have *that* soon.

Anyway, he never had a chance to explain, because at that moment, a pudgy, carrot-haired boy appeared in the doorway. He stared hard at Werner and then said, "Who the hell are you? We don't allow trash like you in this building!"

"Don't speak like that, Norman," said Anika. She squeezed Werner's hand. "He's my friend."

Nathalie appeared next to her brother. "What's going on?"

"Look at Anika's friend," Norman sneered. "He must come from the *old* country."

Nathalie gazed at Werner scornfully. "He sure has old clothes and crummy shoes." She snickered, then turned to her brother. "The way that girl brags about her life in Europe." She mocked Anika's foreign accent. "*The silver, the servants, the fancy dresses.*" Then she turned her gaze to Anika. "Probably all lies!"

Werner could see Anika shrinking from their words. What did they know about her? How much she'd lost? "Don't talk to her like that!" he snapped.

"Hey, you creep," Norman shouted back. "Better scram now before I call the cops!"

For an instant, Werner froze, unable to think, much less speak. He knew that in another second, Norman would pull Anika inside and slam the door. He would be outside; she'd be inside. Locked in that home that was *not* a home, that was anything *but* a home!

He tugged on her hand. "Come with me!"

"What are you saying? Where are you going?" Norman's face grew puffy and pink. He grabbed at Anika's blouse, tearing the thin fabric. "She's not going anywhere! Certainly not with you!"

But in that same instant, Anika pulled away from Norman. Both she and Werner dashed toward a door marked STAIRS, next to the elevator. Neither dared glance back to see if anyone had followed. The two fairly leaped down fifteen flights, several steps at a time, hand in hand. No one seemed to be pursuing. Werner guessed that the Furstburners would take the elevator. He wondered again how fast it went down and if they'd reach the lobby before them.

A moment later, when they rushed into the lobby, Werner glanced over. A stout, white-haired lady with three big black French poodles was trying to squeeze onto the elevator. Good. Until the elevator was free to go up, the Furstburner twins couldn't come down.

Rudolf and the elevator man were busy trying to help the lady with the poodles. They looked up as Werner and Anika raced across the marble floor. The doorman started to follow but tripped on a dog leash. The two shot out the door and headed toward Central Park.

Rudolf followed, waving his arms. "Stop, stop, you crooks!"

But they ran on and on, nearly colliding with roller skaters, baby carriages, and kite flyers. Still they kept going, as fast as possible. Finally, white-faced and panting, Anika crumpled to the ground. "Werner, please, no farther."

On the shiny green grass, she looked like a doll thrown by a careless child. Werner was bent over, too, gulping for air.

The thumping of his heart finally slowed, however, giving him a chance to think. What now? Where would they go? What would they do? Any minute now, the Furstburners would reach the park in search of them. There might be policemen as well.

Anika imagined that Werner had a home, a safe place where she could live, too. How could he tell her the truth? Could he take her down to his tiny apartment on Second Avenue? Werner could imagine the look on her face as she trudged up the dark, smelly stairs in his building. She was accustomed to fine clothes, china, and silver. Why, she'd hate everything about Second Avenue.

But they had to do something quick, before the Furstburners appeared with the police. Werner looked around at the trees, bushes, and boulders. The park was huge. There had to be a million places to hide. Anika and he might last here for days, even weeks, enough time for him to come up with a new plan.

He looked at Anika and caught her studying him.

"You are different, Werner," she said slowly. "You're taller and stronger."

"I guess so," he muttered.

"You look like…," she smiled mischievously, "Huckleberry Finn."

Huckleberry who? What a peculiar name! Werner's hands flew up to flatten down his thick, sandy hair. Probably some bum!

"He's an American boy. And that's why you look like him now. You're American too." Her voice was wistful, like his being American was both good and a little sad. It meant the two had left their homeland for good.

Her strong gaze made him feel shy. "Anika, you sure you don't wanna go back? I bet the Furstburners won't blame you, they'll blame me."

She jumped up like a startled fawn. "No, I don't want to go back! Please, don't make me go back!"

For a moment the two gazed straight at one another like the first time they had met on the ship, when she had cracked open the door and invited him in.

Werner stood up straight and offered Anika his hand. Then they headed deeper into the park, far from their pursuers.

Chapter Twenty-Five

At first, the park was great fun. They nearly forgot that anyone might be searching for them. They discovered a playground with swings, a seesaw, and a slide. They played together like little kids, like the little kids they'd rarely had a chance to be in the past. Anika giggled as she sat on the swing and demanded, "Push me higher, Werner, *higher!*"

A moment later, jumping off the swing, she yelled, "Catch me if you can!"

She started running, and the two chased each other around the trees and bushes. Remembering the joy of rolling down the hill with Sam, Werner shouted, "Look at this!"

He lay down and rolled down the hill, jumping up at the bottom with a grin. Bits of grass stuck to his clothes. "Now you try, Anika. It's fun!"

She stared at him a moment, then shook her head. "*Nein, noch nicht.*"

No, not yet. Anika was still a well-behaved German girl who couldn't act wild and free. Certainly not in public. Werner knew how she felt because he had felt like that once, but no longer. He flicked pieces of grass off his shirt, surprised at how much he'd changed.

Every once in a while he glanced around but didn't see anyone with frizzy orange hair. Nor did he spy Rudolf or the police.

The sun began to set and people started leaving the park. A family packed up their picnic basket and gathered toys and skates. An old couple stood up carefully from the bench where they'd sat feeding pigeons and moved slowly down the path.

Soon only young men and women were strolling around, holding hands, laughing together, and stealing kisses. Werner didn't worry that any of these young couples would notice them. He'd often heard that lovers only have eyes for each other.

As the sky darkened, he and Anika quit playing. They wandered from place to place in the park, following one path and then another. They were cautious, ducking out of the way when they glimpsed anyone. As the light faded and shadows grew, even the kissing couples began to disappear. He figured they might be going for a meal in a restaurant, dancing, or to the movies. Unlike him and Anika, they had places to go.

After a while, the only people still in the park were police on horseback. One police officer, riding on a big grey horse, stopped when he saw them. "Hey, you kids, whatcha doing up so late? Don't your parents expect you home?"

"Yes, officer," Werner said respectfully, turning to Anika. "Gosh, Anna, it is getting late. Mother and Father will be worried. Let's go home straightaway."

"Of course, Willy, let's go," Anika replied quickly. She put her hand in his and began humming a tune as they walked away. As soon as they had rounded a bend, however, she asked, "Do you think he'll tell? I don't want them to find us."

Werner shrugged.

Her lower lip stuck out a bit. "I wish we'd brought something to eat."

Werner looked around. The hotdog and popcorn vendors had all left the park, even if they'd had money to buy something. Poor Anika. It was okay for him – he was used to pangs of hunger – but she'd probably never felt an empty stomach.

They trudged farther. The park seemed to grow bigger as they walked. But it no longer seemed like a magic carpet unfurling at their feet – it was empty and boring. Werner again considered heading back to his old neighborhood. A can of tomato soup would taste mighty good at that moment. Plus Second Avenue wouldn't look so ugly under streetlights.

"Hey, Anika, I was thinking…"

But she suddenly stopped short. "I know where we can go! It will be perfect."

Excited, she began to run, and he followed. Five minutes later, she pointed to a stone building ahead. "Look at that, Werner. Isn't it *wunderbar?*"

He gazed in amazement. "It's a castle, a real castle like in Germany, only much smaller." The castle had stone towers and little arched windows. How incredible to see such a thing in the middle of New York City!

"Let's go in," exclaimed Anika. They rushed up the steps to a wooden door and pulled hard, but it didn't budge. Werner walked all around the building, peering in every window and checking each latch. The castle was locked up tight. He looked at Anika. "Sorry."

She slumped down on the steps, pouting.

Now he didn't dare mention going to Second Avenue. Not when Anika's idea of a wonderful place was a castle! He gazed away from the building over a low stone wall. Below was a lake; its water glimmered softly. In the distance, thousands of lights glittered from tall buildings ringing the park. The lights shone like a distant fairyland, friendly and cheerful. Then the shrill sound of a police car sounded. He shuddered. Were the police looking for them?

Werner sat down next to Anika. "Come on, let's not be unhappy. We could play another game like, like…hide-and-seek."

She pressed her lips together in a sour frown. "That's too *dumm*, Werner – playing hide-and-seek when we're really hiding and someone is really searching for us."

But a moment later, she stood up and the two started walking again, not in any particular direction, just walking. As the night closed around them, they entered a small thicket of trees and bushes. A branch scratched Werner's face, another caught on his shirt. They stumbled over rocks. The path forked again and again, and he chose whichever way seemed right.

"Do you know where we're going?" Anika asked. She was trembling slightly.

He shrugged. "We're not lost, I promise." But at that moment he stepped into a stream; the water quickly soaked his socks. The air was becoming chilly. He could barely hear noises from the city. It seemed as if they were the only live things in the park.

Anika finally stopped. "I won't go any farther."

"Okay," he said. The two sat down, then crawled close to a bush and lay down, side by side. Werner put his arm under Anika's head to form a pillow. A few mosquitoes whined overhead.

"*Mein Gott*, Werner, look at the dancing lights!" she exclaimed. "*Gluhwurmchen* – lightening bugs! I've heard of them but never seen them."

He also marveled. "They're wonderful." He reached up and caught one in his hand, bringing it down close and opening his fingers. The two watched the insect crawl across the palm of his hand, its tiny beam of light going on and off, off and on. Then it flew off. "Like magic," said Werner.

Anika's eyelids were drooping. "What will we do tomorrow?" she murmured.

Werner didn't answer. He didn't know. He turned his head and looked at Anika. Her eyes were closed, her thin body still, her breathing soft. He whispered softly to her, "You are very brave, *Prinzessin*, to sleep here on the hard ground and not complain a bit."

He lay awake longer, shifting to get comfortable amid a few sharp stones and sticks. Yet the earth beneath also felt solid and comforting. He knew there were miles and miles of dirt and rock stretching all the way to the other side of the earth. All the way to Germany. What time was it there now? What were Father and Bettina doing at that moment? When would he see them? Would they come as planned in weeks or months? Everything seemed so topsy-turvy. Yet they would come, that's one thing he now felt sure of.

Werner's eyes were nearly shut when h
scratching noise close by. Turning his head,
dark. Only a few feet away, three furry anim∟
noses and thick striped tails were digging in th
instant, the little creatures stopped their digging
him with glittering red eyes, then scampered off.

Above, the white circle of the moon drifted la2
tree branches. How remarkable, he thought, to be h
Anika in this completely strange place, yet to feel as ⌐
he had felt in a very long time.

Chapter Twenty-Six

That's how he found them. Two kids in grimy clothes curled up under a bush in Central Park. His name was Amos Todd.

As soon as Werner opened his eyes and saw an old colored man peering down, he scrambled to his feet.

"Well, well, well," the old man muttered. "I guess I seen a lot worse than you two." He leaned on the rake he was holding.

Anika began to stir also. "*Wer ist das?*" she murmured, then her eyes widened with fright. Werner knew why. He'd feared black people also until he had made friends with Alf, the gentle giant. Then his attitude had changed and, he figured, it was time for hers to change, too. Werner shook the dirt and sticks from his clothes and reached for her hand. "Come on, Anika. Time to get up."

She stood up, still staring shyly at the old man.

"You kids hungry?" he asked in a friendly voice.

"Oh, yes," Anika exclaimed.

Werner smiled, knowing hunger bests any other emotion.

"Come with me." The colored man gestured and walked slowly. The two followed.

Werner hoped a full stomach might help him think, as his friend Sam often suggested. It was still early, but soon people would start crowding into the park, including policemen. The Furstburners might also appear.

Werner's brain was already working. What would he and Anika do today? Where would they hide?

"My name's Amos Todd," said the old man. "Here's where I work." He pointed to an old gardening shed. A denim jacket hung on a hook inside the shed. From the pocket, he removed several sandwiches and handed them to the two kids.

Just baloney and yellow cheese glued together with mustard between slices of white bread. But food had never tasted so great! Anika and Werner gobbled down the sandwiches. He figured their breakfast had been Mr. Todd's lunch, but the old man didn't seem to mind.

"What's y'alls names?" asked Mr. Todd.

They both spoke at once. Werner stammered, "I'm David and this is Elena" while Anika said, "He's Frank and I'm Sadie."

Mr. Todd's mouth twitched. "That's okay. You don't need to tell me your right names if you don't feel like it."

Something about his easy acceptance of them made Werner feel trusting. "Look, Mr. Todd, you know this park better than we do. And we *uh…*we need some help. Can you show us where to hide?"

The old man didn't seem a bit surprised, as if runaway people often crossed his path. "There's a couple a' places in this park you might stay hid for a while." He pulled at one of his big ears. "Depends on how hard they're looking for you."

Werner glanced at Anika. Her face was smirched with dirt, her hair uncombed, her blouse torn. How different she looked from the elegant girl he'd met on the ship.

"I don't know how hard they're looking," Werner said, "but we don't want to get caught."

"Uh-huh," Mr. Todd slowly nodded. "So, boy, can you use a shovel?"

Werner hesitated a second. He'd never held a shovel in his life. "Sure, I can."

"How 'bout you?" He looked kindly at Anika. "Can you stay a bit on your own?"

Anika pressed closer to Werner, but spoke calmly. "*Ja*, I can."

"Just for a few hours, sweetie," Mr. Todd added, "while your brother here helps me."

Leaving Anika at the shed, Werner followed Mr. Todd to where he was working.

That day Werner learned all about digging a ditch. He learned what hard work it is, lifting one shovelful of dirt after another, then another and another. Until he lost count. The shovel's wooden handle was old and splintery; his palms were soon sore and blistered. The air grew steamy, and his clothes clung to him from sweat. And still the two kept digging.

They worked steadily until the shovel grew so heavy that Werner didn't think he could lift another pile of dirt.

"Time for us to go see your sister," said Mr. Todd, pulling the shovel from the boy's aching hands.

Anika looked much happier than when they'd left her. She had been exploring the shed. "Look what I found!" she exclaimed. She pointed to a corner under the roof where a sparrow had built a nest. The nest was lined with soft feathers and filled with broken shells.

"Those little birds left a while back," said Mr. Todd, "but the same pair come every spring. Or they seem the same." He glanced at Werner who'd sunk down on top of a bag of fertilizer. "Now you two stay here while I fetch us some food." He took off down a nearby path.

"Oh, Werner, isn't this lovely? This could be our little home," Anika exclaimed.

He smiled. In just a few hours, Anika had become a real *hausfrau*, a tidy homemaker. "For just for a little while," she added. "Just 'til Father comes."

"Your father? Have you heard from him?" Werner asked.

"At first, I heard every week. He wrote that he had traveled from Germany to Holland and then to France. But since then, I've heard nothing." Anika's voice faded, and she bit her lower lip. But she quickly perked up. "I know he will get here. I know it!"

Mr. Todd returned with several brightly colored boxes of Cracker Jacks and handed them to the kids. They tore open the boxes and soon both had sticky fingers.

Later, when Mr. Todd and Werner returned to the ditch, the old man said, "A policeman asked if I'd seen a girl and a boy together in the park. Sounded like you two." He plunged the shovel deep into the soft earth, then asked, "You murder anybody?"

"No, sir, we didn't," Werner replied. "I promise."

Mr. Todd spoke no more for a while, but finally he muttered, "Y'all gonna come home with me tonight. That's what y'all gonna do."

At his words, something in Werner's chest lightened. It was like Esther always said, some people find a way to help, any way they can. The old man didn't know them at all and yet he was willing to take them home and keep them safe.

Werner tried to grip the shovel again but his palms were too sore. He gasped out loud in pain. Mr. Todd pulled a ragged red bandanna from his pocket. "Wrap the handle in that, son. It won't hurt you so bad."

Late in the afternoon, Werner told him their real names and how they got to the park. Mr. Todd listened without speaking. During the day, hundreds of people had passed, but none seemed to see them. They were just two fellows, young and old, working on a ditch.

When they returned to Anika hours later, she was curled up asleep on the pile of burlap bags. Her hands were gripped tight in little fists, like she'd been fighting something in her sleep. When Werner touched her, she sat up, and looked around surprised. Then a little frown puckered her forehead. "What will we do now, Werner?"

"Don't worry." He touched her hand. Whatever was ahead, it beat another night in the park.

Chapter Twenty-Seven

Amos Todd knew many paths through the park that were far from the main trails and curious policemen. In minutes, they stood on a wide avenue waiting for the Number 41 bus. Climbing on, Mr. Todd handed the driver a few nickels.

Werner wasn't sure where the bus was going. But he could see that from the street numbers that it was not going back downtown. It was heading farther uptown, toward a strange new part of the city. He stared intently out the window. Soon the streets began looking different. People weren't so dressed up. Cars weren't so new and shiny. More and more Negroes climbed aboard. Soon, from one end to the other, the bus was jammed with dark faces.

Gradually, everyone on the bus began acting like they knew one another. They talked and joked and laughed and shared food. Werner glanced at Anika, who was squeezed next to him on the seat, her body tense.

When the bus stopped at 125th Street, Mr. Todd climbed off and the two kids followed. Their faces were the only white ones on the street.

"Where are we?" murmured Anika in a tight voice.

Mr. Todd smiled. "They call this Harlem."

After a few blocks, they entered a dignified old building. Inside, the rooms were simple but clean and pleasant. Still, Werner wondered what Anika thought – she was used to a revolving glass door, marble lobby, and doorman.

In the rooms, a thin black woman, much younger than Mr. Todd, was carefully folding a pile of freshly ironed laundry into a basket.

"That's my niece Bessie, who looks after me," said Mr. Todd, turning to the woman. "Look who I brung home."

Bessie was clearly surprised at the sight of the two children. But she gave them a warm look. "I bet y'all are hungry? I got some tasty things on the stove ready for supper." She quickly laid out several extra dishes on the table; they were heavy white plates, scratched and nicked.

That night Werner and Anika feasted on creamy mashed potatoes, fried chicken livers, and golden biscuits. They each ate six flaky biscuits, slathering them with butter. There was pie for dessert, a slice of luscious peach pie. Werner hadn't eaten so well in months, not since Esther fell ill. He was glad Anika also seemed to enjoy the hearty meal.

Afterward, Bessie wiped her hands on her apron. "Why, you hungry little birds," she said. "Ain't nothing I like better than feeding hungry people."

Mr. Todd pushed back his chair and slowly rolled a cigarette from tobacco in a little sack in his lap. While Bessie cleaned up the tiny kitchen, he went to the open window and smoked his cigarette.

The only picture on the wall was a flimsy cardboard picture of a man with long, wavy brown hair and blue eyes. He was dressed in a pale yellow robe and around his head floated soft pink and blue clouds. The man's heart had been cut out of his chest and stuck in front of him. It was a huge red heart ringed with sharp thorns.

Anika stared at the picture. "*Was ist das?*"

"That's Jesus," said Werner, who'd seen similar pictures in books and paintings. He didn't know much about Jesus except that he was a Jew. His father had told him when they were passing a statue of Jesus in front of a German church years ago.

"You mean he's Jewish like you and me?" Werner had paused, surprised.

His father nodded, then muttered, "Don't stop here, Werner! Don't you see it's dangerous?"

Werner had glanced at the German families coming out of church at that moment. As usual, he and his father had been hurrying past, their heads low, trying not to be noticed. Even so, a few faces had turned toward them with anger and scorn.

Now Anika gazed intently at the picture of Jesus. "What's wrong with his heart?"

Werner shrugged, but Bessie overheard her question.

"Ain't nothing wrong with *His* heart, honey," she said. "Jesus puts His blessed heart out there like that so we'll know what to do with *our* hearts. Those thorns digging in, that's the meanness and selfishness in the world. He feels the pain we got, the pain we all got."

Anika turned from the picture and looked straight at Bessie. "He knows *everybody's* pain?"

"Yes, honey, He do, He sure do." Bessie was mending a hole in her uncle's shirt. "Your pain and mine, too." Her head was bent low over her sewing.

Anika gazed at Jesus another moment. She was blinking back tears.

Chapter Twenty-Eight

Anika soon fell asleep on a dumpy sofa in the center of the room. Werner stood by the window a short while, gazing out on the street. Along the sidewalk, people were sitting in chairs, talking, laughing, and listening to the radio. He couldn't pick out their dark faces or arms, but their white shirts and light-colored dresses seemed to float in the night. Farther down the block, a tall fellow stood on a corner, playing a trumpet. His horn glinted in the light of a streetlamp above.

Every muscle aching, Werner stretched out on a heavy quilt on the floor. Being in Harlem made him realize that he'd been living in a tiny part of New York. The city was filled with dozens of different worlds. The tough streets of his neighborhood, Anika's world of sleek limousines and perfumed ladies, and now another world of music, food, talk and laughter, as hard-working people stole a little enjoyment for themselves.

It seemed only moments had passed when he felt Mr. Todd's hand on his shoulder, waking him up. He jerked upright, smelling coffee. Bessie was pouring some from a pot into several mugs. Anika was still curled up, fast asleep on the sofa.

"You wanna work with me again, son?" said Amos Todd in a low voice.

Werner's body still ached from the day before. His hands were so blistered you could hardly see the skin. He thought of the police and those nasty Furstburners searching everywhere for him. Wouldn't it be dangerous to go back? Wouldn't it be more pleasant to stay here all day?

But Werner didn't want to sit around eating somebody's food without doing anything. "I'll go," he replied.

"Come git yourself some coffee and biscuits," Bessie called softly. She poured lots of cream in his cup of coffee and set down a plate with warm biscuits and a pile of scrambled eggs.

Werner and Mr. Todd were nearly out the door when Anika woke up. Startled, she called out, "Where are you going?"

"Don't worry, honey," Bessie sat down on the sofa and put an arm around the slender girl. "Us'n will have a fine time today."

Anika's big eyes were the last thing that Werner glimpsed before the door closed. He guessed she was still a little fearful. Spending a day with Bessie, however, might turn her around. That's how it was – you meet one person and they change how you see the world.

Soon he and Mr. Todd were riding the same bus as the day before, now heading toward the park. Digging on the ditch seemed easier today, as if Werner had grown bigger and stronger overnight. His palms were still sore, but the skin over the blisters had begun to harden. It felt as if he could toss more shovelfuls of dirt onto the pile each hour. The ditch gradually grew longer. At midday, Mr. Todd pulled out several sandwiches, and they drank water from a hose. Werner glanced around often, but so far he hadn't seen any policemen searching for Anika and him.

Seated together on the grass, the two chatted a little. Mr. Todd asked about Werner's schooling, and the boy told him about Mr. Pendergrast. Mr. Todd chuckled, "I had a few like that myself."

He explained that he had only managed to stay in school for five years. "My mama died when I was small," he said. "That left my big sister with eight of us to raise. She did a good job with us and with some of her own. Bessie's her daughter."

"Does Bessie have kids, too?" Werner was curious.

Mr. Todd paused. "She had a son, but he ain't with us no more." The lines in his face seemed to deepen. "No, he ain't with us no more."

Werner thought about the heart of Jesus surrounded with a ring of thorns. They each had their own grief – Bessie, Anika, Esther, his own family. He thought of Esther in the big lonely hospital ward. How was she doing now? Was she feeling stronger? Was she even…Werner couldn't think any further. He jumped up, grabbed the shovel, and went back to work. He stayed hard at the job all afternoon. Indeed, the trees were casting long shadows across the grass when the two quit. They put the tools away in the shed and walked to the bus stop.

A few minutes later, standing in line, Werner watched a hefty policeman stroll past. Noticing the boy, the officer stopped short.

Werner gulped, figuring the burly policeman had guessed who he was. In another minute, he'd be arrested and hauled off to jail. Instead, the police officer's voice was overly pleasant. "Whatcha doing in this line, kid?"

Werner stammered. "Huh? What do you mean?"

The cop's mouth slid into a leer. "Come on, kid, you know where this bus is heading. It's heading for Harlem. White people get *off* here at this stop, they don't get *on*."

The officer glanced toward Mr. Todd and the other Negroes waiting in line. "You ain't with any of them, are you?" He was carrying a big thick billy-stick. He thumped it a few times on the palm of his hand. The sound was loud and scary.

For a second Werner couldn't think what to say. His head felt muddled. He just wanted the police officer to go away. "No sir, I'm not," he mumbled. "I'm not with any of them."

The officer nodded with a glint in his eye. "You made a mistake, didn't you? You wuz standing in the wrong line, weren't you?"

Again, Werner had a hard time answering. "I guess so…I guess I am in the wrong line, sir," he muttered, backing away. "Maybe I got mixed up."

The police officer smiled broadly. "That's how it seems to me, kid. Seems like you made a stupid mistake." He started walking down the avenue again, glancing right and then left. He looked like he ruled the street and always had. He called back to Werner. "Don't make that mistake again, kid. Ya hear?"

Werner stood apart from the line of Negroes for several minutes. No one looked in his direction. Then the bus arrived and people began to file on. Mr. Todd was the last in line. There was a heaviness in his step. Finally he called to the boy, "You coming?"

Werner stumbled onto the bus, his head low, ducking past the Negro passengers. He found a seat at the back and sat staring out but seeing little. His head throbbed. A thought ran through his mind over and over. Not everyone in America, this great country, this home to the free, was treated equally. Not everyone. Esther was wrong.

From where he sat, he could see the back of Mr. Todd's grey head. He was glad he couldn't see the old man's face. He remembered when the *Hitler Jugend* had spit at him and forced him to write "dirty Jew" on the pavement. Those boys didn't know his name, yet they hated him. Now Werner realized he wasn't so different. It was easy to hurt others. No matter where you lived, in any country and at any time. You could easily turn toward hate.

He and Mr. Todd climbed off the bus at 125th Street. The two walked in silence with the width of the sidewalk between them. Werner kicked a sharp piece of broken glass off the pavement into the gutter.

After a few blocks, Mr. Todd asked, "You tired as yesterday, son?" Glancing over, Werner saw no trace of hurt or anger in the old man's face. In fact, he looked as dignified as ever, as regal as one of the tall trees in the park.

"No, sir," Werner said, stepping closer to Mr. Todd. "I don't feel nearly as tired."

Chapter Twenty-Nine

When they walked in the door, Anika looked as happy as a puppy.

"We had a good day," Bessie said. "Look at all we got done." She pointed to a high stack of laundry that was clean, pressed, and neatly folded.

"I ironed most of it myself," declared Anika. Her face looked as bright as when they had been together on the ship.

After cleaning up, everyone sat down for a meal. Bessie began serving some meat from a heavy black skillet. "Hope y'all like pork chops," she said. "I got some 'specially fat ones from the butcher today."

Anika instantly pulled her plate away. "None for me," she declared.

Bessie looked surprised. "You don't eat pork chops?"

Werner kicked Anika under the table, but she ignored him. "Of course we don't. We're Jewish."

At her words, Werner felt his body stiffen. He knew Father's words by heart: "Don't tell anyone you're Jewish, not any strangers." Even now, in the United States of America, how could you know how people might react or what they might do if they knew?

Bessie merely spooned the extra chop onto Mr. Todd's plate. "I'll just give y'all some more greens and fried potatoes. I bet y'all would eat that, wouldn't you?"

Anika nodded quickly, and Werner mumbled, "Thanks."

Mr. Todd started to cut up his pork chop but he seemed to be thinking of something else. "I hear you folks is having a bad time of it some places." He forked up a piece of meat while looking at Werner.

Werner stammered. "Y-yes, sir, in Germany where we come from."

"It's horrible." Anika's voice trembled. "Our families are still there."

Mr. Todd was silent for a moment, then glanced at the picture on the wall of the gentle man in a robe. "I never could see how folks could worship one Jew and act so *hateful* to others."

"It don't make good sense," declared Bessie who was standing at the stove. "But there's lots of things in this world don't make good sense."

That night when Werner finally fell asleep, he had a terrifying dream. It seemed as if he were looking through a dark window and he could see Bettina and Father. They weren't at home together as he'd last seen them, however. They were in a forest filled with tall, gloomy trees. His sister was playing her favorite game of hide-and-seek. She was hiding behind a dead tree stump in the woods, a bright smile lighting her face as she waited to be found. Werner started to join the game and pretend to look for her himself. Then he heard someone counting: "*Eins...zwei...drei...vier...*" He glanced back to see who was playing "it." To his horror, he saw Oscar Buddorf sneaking through the forest, searching for Bettina.

"*Nein, nein, Bettina!*" Werner screamed. "*Don't jump out! Stay hidden, please, don't let him find you!*" Though he yelled as loudly as possible, no sound came out....

Waking the next morning, Werner lay on the quilt for several minutes, trying to forget the nightmare. His clothes were damp with sweat. His eyes were still shut when he heard someone crying softly nearby. Opening them, he saw Anika sitting on the sofa, wiping away tears with a hankie.

He sat up. "What's the matter, Anika? What's wrong?"

She looked down at her hands wringing the lace handkerchief. "He won't find me here." Her voice dropped to a whisper. "I'll never see Father again. Never."

Werner's sleepy brain took a moment to figure out what she

meant, and even longer to figure out what they had to do. He thought of all that had happened in the past two days, starting with their escape from the Furstburners, their overnight stay in the park, and their journey to Harlem with Mr. Todd.

Finally climbing off the quilt on the floor, he sat next to Anika on the sofa. She was right, of course. How could her father find her in a place so far from where she had been living? Still, Werner couldn't speak for a moment. Outside, he could hear a few birds calling cheerfully to one another. Mr. Todd and Bessie were still asleep in their bedrooms. At last, he looked back at Anika's tearful face. "It's all right," he said. "When you're ready, we'll go."

She blew her nose into the hankie. "We're going to leave?"

He stood up, stretching. "Yeah, we'll go back to the Furstburners." How he hated even the sound of their name.

Anika smiled and clapped like a child. "Father will come soon. I know he will."

Werner didn't say anything more. He hoped she was right, that her father would come soon and his family, too. But for him, leaving this friendly oasis would not be easy. He liked Mr. Todd and Bessie. Their home was simple and safe. Besides, what did he have to go back to? He had been gone for over three days. Mr. Mozer and Sam must be wondering what had happened to him. Was he lost? Was he dead in some alleyway? In his neighborhood, you often heard stories of people who disappeared or were murdered.

"I like Bessie and Mr. Todd, too." Anika said softly. She reached for Werner's hand. "But we have to go back."

He nodded. "There's no hurry. We'll go after breakfast." He wanted coffee and biscuits. He didn't want to rush off.

Whatever they thought of the decision, Bessie and Mr. Todd didn't make a fuss. Bessie gave them each a big smile and a hug. First Anika was folded into her warm embrace, then Werner. He held on long as possible.

Amos walked with them to the bus stop. As they walked,

Werner wanted to apologize. He wanted to say he was sorry for what he'd said to the police officer. Very sorry. Yet the right words didn't come. Finally, he just thanked Mr. Todd for everything as sincerely as possible. The old man put a hand on the boy's shoulder, his eyes holding an ocean of understanding.

The two kids climbed on the bus and waved good-bye. Anika stared unblinking out the window. Her tense body was tilted forward like she wanted the bus to move faster. Werner wondered how much she had gained from her time with Bessie. He figured some people learn more slowly than others.

When they climbed off, she became even more jumpy. She clearly wanted to cross the park as quickly as possible. Not Werner. He took his time looking at every bush and tree. Vendors were setting up for the day. Several sleepy-looking people were walking their dogs. Werner's feet moved slower and slower until finally the two stood at the street curb. Across the wide avenue, they could see the large apartment building where the Furstburners lived.

Anika stopped and seized his hand. "I never told you why I don't have a mother, did I?" Her voice was shaky.

"You don't need to tell me," Werner replied gently.

"She left us because..." Anika looked away. "Because Father and I are Jewish and she isn't." Anika's voice faltered, then she took a deep breath and continued. "A year ago, I found Mother in my bedroom, packing a suitcase. She said to me, 'You can go, too, Anika. We'll bring all your dresses and shoes. We'll go to Grandmother's village. The Nazis won't find us there. Come with me, darling, come with me.'"

Dozens of cars were whizzing past on the wide avenue. Yet Werner could only see Anika and her mother surrounded by a jumble of clothes, shoes, and suitcases.

"But I couldn't leave him, could I?" Anika's voice was shaky but she shook her head firmly. "Of course I couldn't." She squeezed Werner's hand hard, right on the blisters. "Father will come. I know he will."

Werner turned to her quickly. "You're right, he will."

For a long moment, the two stood there, poised on the edge of the street curb.

"You know what, Anika?" Werner tugged at her hand. "I got a turtle, Julius, somewhere in this park. Maybe we should go look for him."

"Look for a turtle?" The corners of her mouth lifted in a smile. She knew he was stalling for time. She turned away from him and gazed across the street. "You don't have to go with me, Werner. I know the way."

But she didn't drop his hand. The two remained there another minute or longer. To Werner, it felt like a heart-throbbing scene from a movie, when the violin music swells and people sniff into their handkerchiefs. Like when Jane bids farewell to Tarzan because she has to return to civilization and he must remain in the jungle. Except this wasn't a made-up story – it was really happening.

"Hey, you've never been downtown to meet my friend Sam," he started to say. "You'd like Sam and he'd like –"

But at that instant, two cops came racing down the sidewalk toward them. Behind the police was a boy with frizzy orange hair, panting to keep up.

When the policemen grabbed Werner, Norman yelled, "That's right, officer, you've got the kidnapper!"

Werner elbowed one cop in the stomach and jerked to get free from the other. A cop shouted, "Whatcha think you're doing, bud?"

Then Nathalie dashed up, pointing at Anika. "Grab her, too, before she runs away again!"

"Before *she* runs away?" said the policeman who was gripping Werner. He stopped squeezing his arm so hard. "You told us the girl was kidnapped."

"He did kidnap her. He broke into our apartment and stole stuff, too," Norman lied. "But she...she helped him. She told him what to take."

"I did not! How dare you say that!" Anika exclaimed defiantly. Then she turned to Norman and Nathalie. "You want me back?" she declared. "Here I am."

Already, her face was blank. She wasn't going to let the Furstburners know anything – not why she'd left or why she was returning.

Natalie began to pout. "She thinks she's too good for us. Just because she speaks German and French and listens to classical music."

"Let him go," Anika told the policeman still holding Werner. "He never stole anything. Certainly not me." The policeman loosened his grip and Werner pulled free.

"He's a robber and a bum. He belongs in jail!" Norman grumbled. But the police officers just glanced at one another and shook their heads.

"Where you two been?" the cop asked.

Werner knew telling them about Mr. Todd was not a good idea. "There's lots of hiding places, if you know where to look."

"We were just playing games," Anika said, then added deliberately, "and you don't have to worry. I won't be seeing *him* any more." She nodded stiffly in Werner's direction, then quickly looked away.

Werner's heart sank like an anchor tossed into a deep sea. Was this really their last moment together?

Anika stepped off the curb and started across the street. She looked once more at Werner. "*Auf Wiedersehen, alte-Freund.*"

He swallowed hard. She was truly saying good-bye. And indeed they were old friends, even though they'd known each other less than a year. Time was like that now – so uncertain, so troubled – it made you old fast. He watched as Anika walked steadily forward. She held her head high, though her neck seemed as fragile as the stem of a flower.

He called just loud enough for her to hear. "Farewell, princess."

Chapter Thirty

Werner began to run as fast as he could. He wasn't sure where he was running, but he wanted to get away. Away from the cops and far from Nathalie and Norman. If he'd stayed, he might have busted that boy's snotty nose and truly ended up in jail. Nobody ran after him; their attention was on Anika. Soon she would be back in the Furstburner's apartment with the door firmly shut. No chance of sneaking her out again, even if she wanted to go. But she wouldn't leave. She needed to stay where she was, even if she hated being there.

Sometimes the faster you move, the less you hurt....

He tried hard not to think about Anika. About the way the Furstburners treated her like a servant. Of course Anika could survive a little harsh treatment. She looked as breakable as a china teacup, but she wasn't. In her own way, she was as tough as he was.

Suddenly Werner wondered if he was really that tough. He touched his blisters. Though still painful, they were beginning to harden. He thought of Mr. Todd – his hands were deeply calloused, but his heart sure wasn't. No amount of troubles had made him mean and bitter.

At the steps to the subway, Werner stopped and looked around. He noted the shiny automobiles and classy people. Their allure had worn thin for now. He was eager to head back downtown where people were simple, direct, and dependable. Then he'd figure out what to do next. At the bottom of the stairs, he sped past the ticket-taker and jumped the turnstile.

"Come back here, you hooligan!" yelled the man in the booth.

Werner paid him no attention. A minute later, he was lost in the crowd climbing on the train.

When he stepped out of the subway station, it was almost noon. Walking through his neighborhood, he gazed at everything like he'd never seen it before. Nothing seemed the same. It felt like he'd been gone three years, not three days. He counted on his fingers. He'd arrived in the U.S. in late September... now it was early July. Ten months had passed since the day he left the orphanage. How could so much have happened in such a short time?

Walking into Mr. Mozer's store, Werner felt like Robinson Crusoe returning to civilization. Glancing up, Mr. Mozer paused for a second as he counted out change to a tiny white-haired lady. Then he resumed. "Here's $1.24, Mrs. Abramovitz. Thank you." He picked up her sack of groceries and walked with her to the door.

Finally, he turned and faced Werner. "So, *boychik*, you weren't shot, knifed, or run over by a bus?" His bushy white eyebrows rose high on his forehead.

"Nah, none of the above," Werner felt almost cocky.

Mr. Mozer gave him a sharp look. "Maybe I shouldn't ask...."

"You won't learn a thing if you do."

"Well, I can see you're an American now," said Mr. Mozer. "An American smart aleck!"

"Sorry, Mr. Mozer," Werner quickly responded. "It's just hard to say what happened. It's...a little unbelievable."

Mr. Mozer nodded. "Lots of things that happen when you're young are unbelievable."

Werner looked worried. "You didn't find anyone else to do my job, did you?"

The grocer shook his head. "It would be hard to find a good worker like you."

"Thanks." Werner swung around and started to head for the stairs. "I'll come back in a bit and help out." Even returning to an empty apartment seemed like a good idea now. At least his bed was there, his own bed.

He hadn't gone five steps, however, when Mr. Mozer called out. "Wait a minute, Werner. Just one minute. I got something for you." He walked to his cash register and removed something from underneath the counter. Then he walked slowly back toward Werner, gazing down at the bundle in his hands.

"This came while you were away," he said, handing the boy a stack of letters, tied together with string. Thin, pale blue letters. He watched as Werner loosened the string, then thumbed through them, one at a time. The boy examined every envelope, carefully addressed with his own handwriting, as if he'd never seen it before. As if he didn't recognize the address.

Werner didn't need to count. He knew instantly that each and every letter was there. Every single letter that he had written to Father and Bettina from the time he arrived ten months ago to the very last letter he had posted. The long letter about Coney Island that he so looked forward to his father and sister reading. The stack, he guessed, contained over sixty letters in all.

On each was the same official stamp in dark red ink: *EMPFÄNGER UNBEKANNT.*

He knew what that meant: PERSON UNKNOWN. He knew it meant that the person who was supposed to receive this letter was no longer living at that address. His father and sister were no longer living in their home. In the home they had shared for as long as he could remember. It meant they were gone, disappeared, hauled away as other Jews had been taken, no one knew where.

Werner's eyes rested on the envelopes, but he no longer saw them. What he saw were the faces of Father and Bettina. He saw them as they looked on the afternoon he left. He saw them as they looked other times, too, happier times, long ago.

Finally, unable to bear the sense of dread, Werner burst out, "But tell me, where are they? Where is my Father? Where is my sister? I want to know where they are!" His voice grew higher and higher, almost shrill. His face was nearly as pale as Mr. Mozer's apron.

The old man opened his mouth and then shut it. He touched Werner's shoulder. "I don't know where they are. Who knows where they are right now?" he said gently, then added. "But there's hope, always hope, that they have found a safe place."

Hope...hope? To Werner, hope seemed like fluffy goose feathers floating skyward, nothing you could grasp onto or hold tight to. *Where was his family? Where were they?*

All these months he had counted on them reading his letters, learning about Esther, the apartment, his friend Sam, the school, the neighborhood, the United States. He had imagined them pouring over his words, knowing they had a safe place to travel to. He had imagined them preparing for their trip, setting out across the ocean, toward the United States, toward him. But now they were nowhere – they had never read a single word of what he'd written. He hadn't helped them even a tiny bit. He had failed completely. *Where were they?*

He looked at Mr. Mozer and the man could see in the boy's bleak face and hollow gaze that there was no hope. No hope at all.

Werner staggered back a step or two. He reached out to prop himself against the wall, but even that felt thin and flimsy. Like it might topple over any second. He couldn't think what to do next, even the next second. Everything had been held in place by that one thought – his family arriving. And what he must do to make that happen. What if they weren't coming? What if they *never* came?

His mind was still reeling from these awful thoughts when Sam bounded through the door. The moment he glimpsed Werner, a grin spread big across his face. His buddy had gone missing for three whole days – he was thrilled to see him alive – and eager to hear his adventures.

Stepping closer, however, Sam caught the look on Werner's face – dazed, bewildered, stricken, a ghostly remnant of himself – and Sam's grin quickly faded.

He didn't say a word to Werner. He didn't ask about the letters in the boy's hand. Or where Werner had gone for three days or why he'd suddenly come back. The two just stood side by side for a minute, dumb as posts.

Finally, however, Sam couldn't remain still another second. "Hey, Werner, whatcha say we get out of here?"

Werner didn't answer at first because he didn't feel he had a voice. Then he shook his head. "Nah, Sam, I don't want to go no place."

He wanted to add – *because there's no place to go.* That's what he was thinking. No place on earth you could go, no matter how fast you run…that life doesn't sock you in the jaw or kick you in the shins or jab you in the stomach. The dark clouds pursue you…you can't escape them.

He felt stupid even thinking that things could be different. Why did he have so much hope for himself and his family? Life was a thunderstorm in the middle of a clear day, a nightmare, a missed chance to grab the golden ring. Did anyone ever grab the golden ring?

"Come on, pal, things always look different outside," Sam insisted. "You need some air. You look like you haven't been breathing for a while. Another minute with no air and you'll be dead."

Werner shrugged, what difference did it make? "Okay, Sam, we'll go outside." As the two walked out, they passed Mr. Mozer, but he didn't look up. The old man remained hunched over his cash register, looking small and defeated.

Yet Sam was right. Outside was better than inside. Feeling the air and light on his skin made Werner feel more awake. Sam urged him again. "Hey, Werner, I know a place you never been, a new place we can go."

"I don't want to go any place new," said Werner. "I don't

want to go anywhere at all."

"Please, please come with me," Sam begged.

Werner was about to say "no" again, but at that instant he glanced down the street. Who was the last person on earth that he wanted to see? Conrad Bluesteiner, of course – and the short stocky man was heading straight toward him. It didn't take a genius to guess why he was coming this way now. He must have bad news about Esther, and he was getting ready to throw Werner out of the apartment.

Werner couldn't bear hearing any more bad news – *not now,* not on top of everything else.

He turned quickly to Sam. "Let's go."

Chapter Thirty-One

The two immediately set out in the opposite direction from Conrad. Seeing them take off, the guy immediately yelled and started to run after the boys.

But Sam led them at a fast pace. He knew the area well. He cut back and forth between lines of cars and trucks inching down the streets. He skipped through alleys and around garbage cans and piles of trash. He leapt over rubble and broken glass in empty lots and sprinted past men at work. They passed men loading trucks, hanging doors, painting signs. They sped across a bridge spanning a wide highway. Glancing at the cars down below, Werner felt dizzy. But he kept going, following Sam's quick steps.

Once he glanced back and saw that Conrad was no longer behind them.

Finally they reached a big open field. "Come on, Werner, we're almost there," said Sam and they ran as fast as they could.

A minute later, panting for breath, they stood on the edge of a broad stretch of water. "The East River," said Sam, sounding proud, like he'd created it.

"See that bridge?" he pointed. "That's the Manhattan Bridge. "And the one past there, that's the Williamsburg Bridge." The tall steel bridges loomed big and powerful against the sky.

"Guess what's across the river?" Sam asked.

Werner shrugged; he had no idea.

"Brooklyn." Sam's eyes lit up. "I got an aunt and uncle in Brooklyn and lots of cousins. Someday we're gonna live over there." His face shone with the happy thought.

Werner looked east toward Brooklyn. But he wasn't thinking about the peaceful island filled with big families, nice houses, schools and playgrounds. He was thinking about what was on the other side of Brooklyn – the Atlantic Ocean. And what was on the other side of that ocean. He was thinking of guns firing, bombs exploding, women and children screaming and trying to hide, soldiers bloody and dying. All that bad stuff was happening, you just couldn't see it from here.

Sam opened his arms wide. "The East River is one great river, ain't it?"

The two were standing on a wooden pier twenty feet above the water. Werner could see the swift currents moving past, dragging bits of wood and trash. In the middle, a green tugboat pulled a heavy barge sunk deep in the water, moving so slowly it hardly seemed to move at all. Above their heads, a single white gull flew past, its bright beady eye glancing down at them. A breeze loosened the air.

"I like it here," Sam said. He glanced at Werner, hopefully. He'd done the best he could, bringing his best friend to his favorite spot. "I come here myself when I'm outta sorts and things aren't going right." Sam stared at the river. "Something about the sky and water makes me see myself small and the world big." He looked at Werner and shrugged. "Sometimes, that helps."

Werner didn't speak for a moment. He knew that Sam was trying to make him feel better. And he wished he could feel better. He wanted to believe that somehow everything in their lives – especially for the people they loved – was going to be all right. But as much as Werner wanted to believe that, he didn't, not at all.

Sam turned to Werner and his eyes now held a question. He wanted to know where his friend had been for three days. What had happened? Had it been terrible or terrific?

Werner tried to speak. He wanted to tell Sam about rescuing Anika, how the two had escaped to Central Park, about

Mr. Todd and going to Harlem and everything. It had been an exciting three days, a real adventure. Probably no kid from their neighborhood had ever done anything like that!

Yet Werner's brain wasn't working right. Everything seemed a blur – Sam, the pier, the barge beyond. His legs didn't feel like they belonged to him. They couldn't support his weight. And his feet weren't connected to the pier any more. They weren't connected to anything.

Inside, a part of him seemed to collapse, like a kite losing wind that dives to the ground. Swaying, he reached out, but found nothing to grasp onto.

Darkness flooded his head. Very faintly, he glimpsed Father and Bettina, their faces set in the tender frame of childhood, but gradually slipping away, further and further away. Then he fell…down, down, down…surrounded by a swirl of thin blue envelopes….

A second later, embraced by cold water, Werner gasped for air and struggled to reach the surface. The river's dark swift current, however, dragged him down. He sank deeper and deeper until his mind, his muscles, his heart seemed to give way, to *give up*….

"Werner, Werner, grab on!"

He heard Sam's voice faintly like a distant echo. His friend's fingers grazed his cheek. A few feet away in the water, Sam was reaching toward Werner with one arm while thrashing with the other to stay afloat. But, by now water was streaming into Werner's mouth and nose, trickling down his throat and creeping into his lungs. In another moment, the boy Werner Berlinger would be *drowned* – gone, gone forever from this life!

Yet in that same instant, Werner felt as if his chest was being squeezed in the fist of God. With all remaining strength, with his arms and legs desperately flailing, Werner pushed himself up to where water and light meet. Spitting out a mouthful of grimy water, he cried, "Sam!"

A second later, his friend's free arm had locked around him, pulling the two close. And they started swimming together, though Werner was half-drowned and Sam had to do most of the paddling. Still, the powerful river was carrying them past some pilings and a pier, towards the ocean.

Werner was too weak to yell, but Sam shouted, "Help! Help us!"

Above on the pier, someone spotted the two struggling boys. A thick rope was thrown down and both grabbed for it. "I'm pulling you out, boys," a voice called. "Hold tight."

The two were dragged out. Werner lay flat on his back for several moments, eyes shut. Beneath him were cool wooden planks. Above, someone was pumping his chest, pushing down over and over again, until water gushed from his nose and mouth.

"You look alive, kid," the man grunted and stood up.

Werner could only open his eyes a slit, but it was enough to see who was staring down at him. His jaw sagged open in surprise. Conrad stood above, his short stocky legs planted firmly on the pier. *What the hell was he doing here?* The man's little eyes gazed intently at him without a word. Then Conrad reached down, grasped Werner's hand and pulled him to his feet. The boy swayed a moment, dizzy and unsure.

"Watcha doing, jumping in the river like that, kid?" Conrad grumbled. "Ya wanna git wet, open up the fire plug. That's what we kids used to do."

Minutes later, Conrad drove the boys back to Second Avenue in an old truck. He gripped the steering wheel as he talked. "I wuz looking all over fer you, Werner," he explained. "Then, just when I spot you and your buddy, you take off for God-knows-where. I can't keep up with the running, so I borrow this truck from a fella to follow."

He pulled up in front of Mr. Mozer's store. "And when I finally git there, you nearly drown yourself to death."

Werner glanced over. Conrad's face was cloudy with emotion. He clearly wanted to say more, but was having a hard time squeezing out the words. When Werner started to climb out of the truck, however, Conrad caught his arm. "Heard you went missing for a few days."

Werner muttered, "Yeah, I did."

Conrad eyed him sternly. "You don't need to do that any more. You don't need to run off anywhere." He turned his gaze back to the steering wheel, still frowning. "What I said about sending you back…I wouldn't a done it, you know? I never woulda done it."

Werner slammed the truck door. "Thanks." That's all he could manage at the moment.

Without another word, Conrad gunned the truck and sped down the street. Werner stared after him dumbly. Was that truly all the short man had to say to him? He still hadn't explained *why* he was looking for Werner. But the boy didn't need his explanation. He knew what Conrad had planned to say. Once he saw what poor shape Werner was in, however, even Conrad had shown mercy. He hadn't spilled the bad news. And, thank God, he had reached the river when he did. If he hadn't….

Sam looked at his friend closely. "You all right?"

Though still unsteady, Werner nodded.

"Maybe I should go up with you, huh?"

Werner shook his head. "I'm okay." He wanted time on his own. He had to think what was next. Even without the threat from Conrad, he was unsure what to do. How he'd live there on his own. Without even a bird or turtle for company…and most of all without the goal of seeing his family, of getting a foothold in this new country, so they'd follow.

The plunge in the cold East River had waked him up, for sure, but it hadn't cured him of his misery, his sense of losing everything that mattered.

Sam gazed at his pal another moment, then turned and headed off, ever quick and light on his feet. Werner watched him go. Sam must have dived in a second after he tumbled off the pier. His friend hadn't given any thought to what might happen to *him* in the mighty river. Walking jauntily away, Sam's clothes were still soaked and filthy, but on him they looked like princely garb.

Trudging upstairs, Werner could feel the stairs beneath his feet. Each step felt as if he were lifting the weight of centuries. Around him, the air reeked as usual of boiled cabbage and fried onions. He was tired, damp, sore, and *alone*. Yet even in his aloneness, he felt close to everyone he had ever cared about. Mother, Father, Bettina, Esther, Mr. Todd, Anika – each would stay in his heart as long as he lived.

The river hadn't done its deadly work. He had escaped – he was the lucky one. Werner stumbled and reached for the rail. He hadn't succeeded in saving anyone, only himself. But wasn't that something? He recalled his father's words: "*Werner, please understand. You must go. It's the best chance you have – to stay alive. That's what counts now. All that counts.*"

Indeed, he was alive now to feel the shock, grief, delight, joy, and everything that makes being alive what it is – a triumph over darkness, a reaching out for...

He stopped short. The apartment door was slightly ajar. Inside were sounds, familiar sounds...

As Werner pushed open the door, a playful breeze washed over his face. Across the room, he saw Esther, seated in her wheelchair under the window – so thin and frail, it seemed a shaft of sunlight might cut right through her. Yet seeing Werner – damp and forlorn – her face flushed with pleasure. She lifted trembling hands in his direction, her voice filled with gladness.

"Werner, dearest, they said I was all mended and could come home," she murmured. "Conrad brought me here today. When we didn't see you, I sent him to find you."

A warm smile spread across her face. "It's *wunderbar*, isn't it, Werner? Being home."

Above her, Mozart's bright song spread through the room.

Epilogue

A little over a month later, on September 7, 1940, Nazi bombers began shelling London, and Werner's school P.S. 122 opened for the new school year.

When he got back to school, he learned that Mr. Pendergrast wasn't teaching fourth grade any more. "He's moved to Connecticut," the principal explained to any student who asked. "I think he'll be happier there." Every kid wanted to cheer but nobody did. They all just looked at one another and winked.

The big news came a little more than a year later, on December 7, 1941. The American military base, Pearl Harbor, had been bombed. The United States immediately entered the war, first against Japan and then Germany. Though it was a big shock to many, Werner was jubilant. Beating the Nazis mattered to him more than anything. And only his country, the United States of America, had the power to defeat the German army. Otherwise, the Nazis might turn the whole world into the dark, evil place Germany had become.

After receiving the bundle of returned letters, he never wrote Father again. But he never quit thinking of his family. He believed it was possible something lucky had happened and that they were safe and sound, too. Werner realized how fortunate he'd been to make it alive to America. Thousands of Jews and many others had been eager to leave Europe. But few had made it. Of the neighbors Esther had helped prepare documents for, only Mr. Boronski's niece Sofia and David Sesselbaum's sweetheart Nancy were able to get to the U.S.

Esther remained frail, and Werner continued to work

diligently to keep her healthy. Yet now Conrad and he were allies in this task rather than adversaries. Mozart kept up his bright song, and often the apartment was filled with the delicious odor of Nudel kugel.

After America got in the war, patriotic Germans like Oscar Buddorf weren't popular in the neighborhood. Not at all. One day his tobacco shop was there, and the next it was boarded up with a "For Lease" sign in the window. Nobody could say exactly where he went. Someplace, guessed Werner, where people like him were more welcome.

He did see Anika again. He was a senior in high school, working two jobs – weekdays after school for Mr. Mozer, and weekends washing windows for a big company. Mostly he worked uptown on the windows of department stores and office buildings. One warm afternoon, he was washing the windows of a popular restaurant named Schrafts. It was a favorite spot for people who could afford the fancy sandwiches, salads, and huge ice cream sundaes. While sudsing the window, Werner spied a lovely young lady sitting in a booth. Although she'd grown a lot, he immediately recognized Anika's delicate face and proud manner. Her clothes were new and fashionable, a mint green dress with a lace collar that set off her dark curls.

Across the booth from Anika was a tall distinguished gentleman, his dark hair streaked with grey. The man was stooped in the shoulders as if he carried a big weight. He looked far older and sadder than he had four years before, but Werner knew right away that he was Anika's father. A bright smile lit up her face every time she glanced up at him. The two were spooning up hot fudge and whipped cream from two giant sundaes. Werner gazed wistfully at the pair. Anika's father had made it to the United States, just as he promised he would.

For a moment, Werner put down his wet rag, thinking that he'd go in and say hello. Then he paused. A young guy wearing grubby work clothes didn't belong in Schrafts! Anika would probably feel embarrassed to see him. She was a proper young lady now. Had she ever told her father about running away from the Furstburners? Or about their hiding in Central Park and going to Harlem? Werner didn't think so. And why should she? Her story had a happy ending....

Suddenly, Anika glanced towards the window. Her eyes seemed so warm and friendly, Werner thought for a second she'd seen him. But then she looked back at her father and took another spoonful of sundae, dripping with hot fudge. No, it wasn't the right moment to go in and say hello and shake hands with Anika's father. Not on that day. Yet, somehow, Werner felt certain, without any doubt at all, that one day he'd have another chance to meet with Anika – when his wallet was fat with dollar bills and he was wearing a decent suit of clothes! That would be a happy day for them both!

He never did see Amos Todd again. Once or twice, visiting Central Park, he glimpsed a dark figure amid the trees. But it always turned out to be the shadow of a proud elm or sturdy maple, not that fine old man.

As the war dragged on, Werner grew eager to join the U.S. Army and go fight the enemy. He wanted a chance to come face to face with the Nazi menace that had blighted so many lives. Not just his, but countless people across Europe.

The day his eighteenth birthday arrived, Sam and he headed down to the draft board office on 42nd Street and Lexington. That's where the two ate their first army grub. Days later, both were in uniform. They did a quick course of Army Basic Training in Alabama. Some young recruits had a hard time, but it seemed like a piece of cake for Private Werner Berlinger and Private Sam Ublentz. Then the two headed across the Atlantic on a giant troop vessel. Halfway there, however, the big news arrived. It was May 7, 1945 – the Germans had surrendered. The war was over. In Times Square, New York City, thousands of people cheered and kissed one another.

Their troop ship, however, kept plowing through the waves

toward Europe. Arriving in France, they soon saw what the war had been like – bombed out factories, shops, farms and houses. Thousands of starving men, women, and children roaming the roads.

The first time Werner saw a Nazi soldier up-close, he froze. The terror from his past still haunted his dreams. Only now, the Americans were in charge and the Nazis weren't. Most threw down their weapons and tore the swastikas from their uniforms. They no longer wanted to fight and begged to go home. Werner looked this guy in the eyes. He was blonde and blue-eyed like the boys who had spit at him years ago and forced him to write "dirty Jew" on the pavement.

Werner held a gun to his head. The soldier was terrified; his forehead wet with sweat. He stammered and fell to his knees. "Let me go," he pleaded in German. "Please, let me go home." A huge, fierce anger welled up in Werner. He wanted to punch or kick the guy or even shoot him. Fortunately, Sam grabbed his arm and squeezed it tight. Werner slowly lowered his weapon and the guy ran off.

His job in the U.S. Army was handing out cans of soup, tins of meat, and chocolate candy bars to hungry families. It was good work – and there were thousands to feed in France, Holland, Italy, and Germany. One day a German girl of about twelve with hair so blonde it looked pink in the sun, stood in front of him with an open hand. He handed her a candy bar, and she smiled slightly and murmured *"Gott segnen Sie."* God bless you. Werner watched as she ran off to share the chocolate with other skinny kids. Not all Germans were bad, he thought. Some had helped him stay alive.

Sam got a much, much more difficult job. He was one of the U.S. soldiers sent in to open up the concentration camps. That's where Hitler had put the everyone he hated – mostly Jews but also communists, homosexuals, gypsies, and many others. Most who went in never got out. Opening up those camps was like pulling the lid off the sewer pipes on

Second Avenue on a hot summer day. That used to make the whole neighborhood stink. But the horrid smell from the concentration camps was much worse – it filled the world with an awful stench that has never entirely gone away.

Sam took his job so seriously that his smile disappeared for months. He tried telling Werner what they had found, but Werner didn't want to hear. Each week, however, when lists of concentration camp survivors arrived, he rushed over to read the names. He searched for his family until tears of disappointment blurred his sight.

Part of him knew that the truth was not on any list.

Finally, one afternoon, Sam talked him into going with him to work. Werner only got a few feet beyond the entrance. Stuff was piled high as a mountain: suitcases, clothes, shoes, toys, wallets, watches, walking canes, books, false teeth, jewelry, photographs, umbrellas. A few soldiers were going through the pile, carefully sorting it out. They put the shoes one place and the false teeth in another. Werner wondered why they bothered, the stuff didn't belong to anybody any more.

He decided to leave and called to his friend. "Hey, Sam, see you later.

But as he turned to leave, Werner spied something on the ground. Something so small, most people would never have noticed it. A china doll's head with a few reddish gold hairs still stuck on top. The head had a pretty, painted porcelain face, now muddy and scratched. Werner picked it up and rubbed off the dirt. The face was perfect except for a tiny chip off the nose and a crack in the head that had been carefully mended.

For a long, long time, Werner stood without moving, his heart exploding into a thousand tiny bits in his chest. What should he do now? Drop the doll's head onto that pile where it belonged with the thousands of other things? The things once owned by boys and girls, their mothers and fathers, their uncles and aunts, grandfathers and grandmothers. Thousands and thousands of families that were no more. Surely the doll's head belonged in that pile.

Or should he hurl it as far as possible into the open blue sky? Throw it with the strong arm he'd gained from lifting Esther into her wheelchair, carrying boxes of cans into Mr. Mozer's store, and shoveling dirt with Amos Todd on that long deep ditch.

His life hadn't been easy and not always fun. Some might say he'd had a pretty tough time of it…and yet it was a life. His life. In a year or two, he'd return to the United States, to his home with Esther. He'd probably go to college and then look for work. Someday he might pursue his dream of going out West, to the open plains and high mountains and fast rivers. Maybe Sam would go with him.

In other words, Werner had a whole world of possibilities ahead of him. He could do any of the great and ordinary things people do in their lives. The things that the people who owned the stuff in that giant pile of stuff would never get to do. Not on this earth. Not Father or Bettina.

For a second he felt the touch of his sister's fingers on his chest, the way she held him that last moment, before saying good-bye. Then he realized God had thrown something in his path – a small precious memento. Something to remind him that disappointment and hatred often seem to rule the world, yet never conquer it entirely. Not the way love grips us forever….

He'd had a lot of luck, not just once but again and again. A guy as lucky as he must keep going – he has to. Sticking the little head in his pocket, Werner walked back down the road. Sam saw him leave and waved, but Werner couldn't see through his tears. He just kept going.

He went back to his job of handing out food to hungry people. That was his work for now, and you do whatever you can to help. He'd learned that from Esther.

Author's note

Forced Journey: The Saga of Werner Berlinger is entirely fictional.

The story was inspired, however, by the late Professor Hal Marienthal, who spoke of coming to the United States on his own with nothing but the clothes he was wearing. He was adopted by a family in Chicago.

I was further inspired by the true accounts of 1,400 Jewish children who fled Nazi Europe and came to the United States. You can learn more at www.onethousandchildren.org. Another source of information is *Don't Wave Goodbye: The Children's Flight from Nazi Persecution to American Freedom*, edited by Philip K. Jason and Iris Posner (Praeger, 2004).

Unfortunately, the description of the difficulties that Jews encountered in trying to leave Nazi Germany and come to this country is accurate. The quota for admitting Jews and other European immigrants was slashed in half while the application forms and requirements were greatly increased.

In *Forced Journey,* Werner writes to President Roosevelt's wife, Eleanor, urging her to help. In 1938, Mrs. Roosevelt did privately back a Congressional resolution that would have allowed 10,000 Jewish children to enter the U.S. – similar to the *Kindertransport* that was enacted by Great Britain and allowed 20,000 young people under the age of 16 to enter the country. (Though small compared with the 1.5 million children murdered by the Nazis, it was the most generous act of any country in the world.)

Mrs. Roosevelt's resolution died in Congress, however. The opposition against allowing more Jews to enter the United States, at this time, was too strong. So, only about 1,400 unaccompanied Jewish minors were able to find a safe haven in the U.S. Many of these children were welcomed into loving homes across the country. Others encountered difficulties like Werner experiences in *Forced Journey*. Some of these children were reunited with their parents during or after the war. Others never saw their families again.

Nothing I could write truly conveys the heartbreak experienced by these children who left everything behind during that terrible era to come to the United States. And yet they survived. Most became U.S. citizens and, as Henry Frankel points out in the Foreword, many contributed significantly to this country.

Their stories of loss and resilience are replicated in every era. Generations of young people – from Cuba, Vietnam, Iran, Sudan, and other nations – have fled their homelands to find safety in the United States. Many are still coming today. Like Werner and Anika, these youngsters make a forced journey toward safety and hope.

About the Author

PeterWeiss

Rosemary Zibart has worked as a journalist, playwright and children's book writer. Her newspaper and magazine articles have tackled such issues as how art can transform the lives of at-risk teens and how the Heart Gallery promotes the adoption of children and teens. As a playwright, she has written award-winning plays for adults and children. *Forced Journey: The Saga of Werner Berlinger* is the second in the "Far and Away" series about children impacted by World War II. Rosemary lives in Santa Fe, New Mexico. Learn more about her at www.rosemaryzibart.com.